"I, uh…I stopped and picked up a pizza on the way home. We could share it. If you really wanted to show me those notes… now." Could he sound any less inviting?

Olive smiled. "No thanks. I already ate, but maybe some other time."

"Yeah. Sure." He didn't have to sound so relieved.

She started back toward the house. He slipped his hand into his pocket and found a napkin he'd shoved in there while handing out ice cream at Brody's. "Olive, wait."

She stopped and swung back around. "Yes?"

He held out the napkin. "You've got paint—" he pressed an index finger to the end of his nose "—right there."

"Thanks." She shrugged and shifted the paint can.

"Wait. Let me."

He took the napkin in one hand and cupped her chin with the other. Her skin was soft and when he angled her head, he got a whiff of something. Lavender? For a moment he stood frozen with her chin trapped by his hand, her breath on his fingers. He stared into her eyes and noticed a darker gold ring around the irises.

His gaze drifted to her mouth. Her very desirable, kissable mouth. All he had to do was lean forward to put his lips to hers—

* * *

SMALL-TOWN SWEETHEARTS:
Small towns, huge passion

Dear Reader,

Recently during an interview, I was asked if I wrote scenes to suit my story's theme or for readers' reactions. I confessed I had never thought in those terms. I simply tell the story my characters want told. Oh, I'm sure things like themes are buried deep in my subconscious, but it's probably best not to go poking around in there.

Talking about ideas is easier. They're sparked by something I've heard or read. Like those ads you see on Facebook that say, "You could win a charming B and B!" But ideas don't become a story until the right character steps up to help me tell it. Luckily, Olive saw an ad and was intrigued enough to enter.

I hope you enjoy finding out what happens to Olive when she wins. It might be a case of "be careful what you wish for," or it might lead to everything she's ever longed for. Enjoy finding out!

Carrie

The Hero
Next Door

CARRIE NICHOLS

HARLEQUIN
SPECIAL
EDITION

HARLEQUIN®
SPECIAL
EDITION™

Recycling programs
for this product may
not exist in your area.

ISBN-13: 978-1-335-40843-3

The Hero Next Door

This edition published by arrangement with Harlequin Books S.A.

For questions and comments about the quality of this book, please contact us at CustomerService@Harlequin.com.

Harlequin Enterprises ULC
22 Adelaide St. West, 41st Floor
Toronto, Ontario M5H 4E3, Canada
www.Harlequin.com

Printed in U.S.A.

Carrie Nichols grew up in New England but moved south and traded snow for central AC. She loves to travel, is addicted to British crime dramas and knows a *Seinfeld* quote appropriate for every occasion.

A 2016 RWA Golden Heart® Award winner and two-time Maggie Award for Excellence winner, she has one tolerant husband, two grown sons and two critical cats. To her dismay, Carrie's characters—like her family—often ignore the wisdom and guidance she offers.

Books by Carrie Nichols

Harlequin Special Edition

Small-Town Sweethearts

The Marine's Secret Daughter
The Sergeant's Unexpected Family
His Unexpected Twins
The Scrooge of Loon Lake
The Sergeant's Matchmaking Dog
The Hero Next Door

This one is dedicated to Jo Grant,
who restored my confidence; and to the
best sprint partners ever, Lucy, Pippa, Rachael,
Traci and Aleks; also my Mermaid Masterminds,
Alison, Elizabeth, Jaycee, Kari, Layla and Melonie;
and my always patient beta reader, Marcia.
I couldn't have done this without all of you!

Chapter One

Olive Downing reached for the door leading into the pub-style restaurant but stopped before making contact with the handle. Instead of opening the door, she rubbed her sweaty palms down the front of her jeans.

Quit stalling, she ordered herself. *My life 2.0 isn't going to start itself.*

She opened the door and stepped into the vestibule. Judging by the muffled sounds of music, conversation and clinking of dishes and glasses coming from inside, this place was perennially popular, even on a Tuesday night.

Glancing briefly back over her shoulder at the outer door, she inhaled, then stepped into the chaos of Hennen's, with its scents of burgers, onions and fries. Voices raised in conversation and canned soft rock played in the background.

Being invited to join a group of friends for a casual dinner might not seem like much, but making new friends had never come easy to Olive and, at thirty-three, she had found that the process hadn't gotten any easier over the decades. Her new job as activity director for Sunshine Gardens Senior Living Center had brought her in contact with the center's nurse practitioner, Ellie McBride. Ellie had kindly extended tonight's invitation to Olive, who had just moved to the small town of Loon Lake, Vermont, after winning a house in a once-in-a-lifetime contest. The other woman had been kind and approachable, but Olive still found her heart pounding and her breath hitching in her chest in nervousness.

Olive spotted Ellie across the room and her coworker must've seen her, too, because she jumped up, said something to the others seated at the table and rushed across the room to greet Olive.

"I'm so glad you came." Ellie took Olive's arm and guided her toward the table, nodding and waving to others in the dining room, none of whom Olive recognized. "Everyone is looking forward to meeting you. We saved you a seat next to Cal. Calvin Pope, that is. He's back from training and officially Loon Lake's new fire marshal, so we've made him the man of the hour tonight."

Ellie had invited her to a celebration. Olive wasn't sure what that meant, but she decided to be pleased to be included. "But didn't you tell me Liam was the fire marshal?"

"He was." Ellie's face took on a glow as she glanced toward her handsome husband. "Liam is Loon Lake's newest fire chief."

"Oh, wow, that's wonderful. Congrats to Liam."

"Thanks." Ellie approached a table with six other people crowded around laughing and chatting.

Olive envied the easy camaraderie everyone in the group seemed to have. She'd once been a part of a similar group, back when she and Kurt had been a couple, before they'd called off their engagement. After the breakup, many of their friends felt compelled to choose sides and Olive wasn't always the winner. As a result, she'd felt isolated and wanted to create a new life for herself…away from those people who'd sided with her ex and away from Kurt himself.

Don't start taking a trip down memory lane, she admonished herself. *Leave the past where it belongs.* She'd come to this quaint town in central Vermont for a fresh start and she couldn't do that while dragging the past behind her like overstuffed luggage.

"Let me introduce you to everyone," Ellie said and gave Olive's arm a reassuring squeeze, as if she'd sensed her nervousness. Olive glanced appreciatively at her coworker…and new friend?

"You met Liam the other day at work, so we can skip him," Ellie gushed.

"That's how you can tell you've made it. When you need no introduction." Liam stood and gave a mock bow, causing the others to groan. His glance bounced around the table at his friends. "Hey, show some respect," he joked. Turning to Olive, he said, "Nice to see you again."

"You, too. And congratulations," she told him, and at his startled look, she clarified, "Ellie told me the good news."

"She did?" Liam gave his wife a puzzled frown.

"I told her about you becoming the town's new fire chief," Ellie said in a meaningful way.

"Right," Liam said, nodding his head and smiling.

Olive wondered at the exchange between husband and wife. Had she and Kurt ever had that type of silent communication? She soon found her attention drawn back to the table when Ellie motioned to her.

"Everyone, this is Olive."

Ellie introduced everyone. "That's Liam's sister, Meg McBride Cooper, and her husband, Riley Cooper," she said, gesturing to a pretty redhead and a gray-eyed man. Nodding at a man with his arm around a brunette, she added, "That's Brody and Mary Wilson. And last but not least, here is Cal Pope."

"The new fire marshal," Olive said and nodded

at the man, who jumped up and pulled out the chair next to him.

Olive's heart kick-started. Not only did he have manners, but he was also gorgeous. She was a respectable five feet eight inches, but still had to tilt her head back to meet his gaze. And… *Oh, my,* she thought, staring up at those wide shoulders, unkempt ebony hair and deep-set, dark brown eyes that crinkled in the corners.

Was this a simple get-together with friends or some sort of setup, since everyone else was paired off? She couldn't decide how she felt about that. Nor did she know whether to thank Ellie or be frustrated with her if this was indeed an attempt at matchmaking.

Either way, she admitted, she had to applaud Ellie's taste.

She sat on the chair Cal had pulled out. He took his seat and she smiled, murmuring her thanks to him. He frowned briefly, for some reason, before slowly returning her smile. She may have missed the evanescent negative expression had she not been studying his features. What was that about? Had she done something to annoy him? Or was he wondering the same thing she was, speculating that Ellie might be trying to set them up with one another? If so, he apparently didn't approve—of Ellie's attempts, or of Olive herself?

As she exchanged the usual getting-to-know-you

small talk with the others, Olive remained acutely aware of the brooding man sitting next to her.

"Olive, did I mention that Cal is also one of your neighbors?" Ellie leaned forward to glance down the table.

"Oh?" Olive turned to him and those brown eyes sent a tingle through her. That intense gaze was raising the hairs on the back of her neck. She swallowed. "Which house is yours?"

"The blue Cape Cod across the street from you," he said.

He was close enough she could smell his spicy scent. She realized that if she shifted her thigh slightly, hers would be touching his. She recalled that brief frown when she'd first sat down next to him. Did he think she was in on the matchmaking attempt, if that's what this was? Under the guise of getting herself settled at the table, she scooted the chair away from his as much as she dared without being obvious. She didn't want to appear too forward in front of strangers. "I wasn't sure that house was occupied since I hadn't noticed anyone coming or going in the month since I moved in."

"That's because I've been away for that training Ellie just mentioned." He glanced down at the newly increased distance between their seats.

Had she insulted him by moving her chair? That hadn't been her intention, but she stood her ground. "That's right. Didn't you recently take Liam's job?"

Cal glanced at Liam and back to her. "Well, it's not like I stole it or anything. Liam got a big promotion."

"Yeah, I guess being fire chief is better than…" *For crying out loud, Olive, stop talking!* she scolded. She hadn't intended to imply he'd taken something that he hadn't earned, but to her ears, that sure had sounded like what she'd meant.

"Go on," he said, his lips twitching. "You were saying being fire chief is better than…?"

God, talk about feeling gauche, like being back in high school trying to fit in at a lunch table in the cafeteria, or at least not call attention to herself. And failing miserably. She'd never been the type of person who liked being the center of attention. That could lead to questions about her situation. She'd confided in someone she'd thought was a friend in high school, but the other girl's response was to spread the information and act as if Olive's circumstances had been her fault. After that, boys had taken more notice of her, but she suspected their interest wasn't altruistic.

Her savior appeared in the form of a waitress. Tiffany, according to her name tag, glided up and stood in the narrow space between her and Cal. "Can I get you something to drink before I take food orders?"

She was tempted to order a bottle of…something alcoholic—anything to dull the awkwardness. But she was driving home later, and Olive knew that she was not exactly a drinker. "A diet cola, please."

Tiffany nodded but hadn't taken her gaze off Cal. A sliver of irritation slid down Olive's spine, which she did her best to shake off. "How about a refill?"

"I haven't finished this one yet," Cal said and watched the waitress saunter away before turning back to Olive. "Where were we?"

"I was admiring your house earlier," she said, hoping to reset the conversation.

"You were? Funny, but I seem to remember you just disparaging how I got my job. So what makes my house so attractive?" He picked up his soft drink and took a sip, studying her over the rim of the glass.

Busted. "I apologize, but I sometimes suffer from foot-in-mouth disease. I'm happy that you got a new opportunity." She adjusted her napkin in her lap. "But I really do like your house. Did you have the exterior painted recently?"

He set down his glass. "Actually, I spent the better part of last year renovating it myself. Inside and out."

"A *year*?" She shuddered. "I hope that doesn't portend how long it's going to take me. I'm looking forward to eventually getting the B and B up and running."

"I did most of the work myself, so it took longer than if I'd hired it done. Was reopening the place as a B and B part of the terms and conditions?"

He was obviously referring to the contest she'd won. No surprise there. Everyone in town knew about it and people stopped her on the street or in the supermarket to inquire about it. Not that she could blame them. That contest was the only reason she was the proud owner of an impressive Queen Anne Victorian home in Loon Lake. The previous owner, an eccentric woman in her nineties, had laid out strict terms in her will that the home she'd once run as a B and B be given away as a prize to the person who'd wrote the most heartfelt essay. It was purported that Sadie Pickard insisted on the contest because she feared her heir would repurpose her beloved home. Many of the Victorians around town had been turned into offices. The rules stated the winner had to live in the home and couldn't subdivide it by turning it into offices or apartments. Olive learned the woman's greatnephew had fought the will's terms, but, in the end, had to acquiesce or lose out on his aunt's other assets. Olive still had to pinch herself that she'd been chosen the winner. Writing the essay had been easy. She'd fallen in love with the property the minute she'd seen the picture. Unfortunately, the reality of the house had been a far cry from the photo in the advertisement. The fact the place had sat empty while the great-nephew fought over the will hadn't improved its condition.

Even after moving into the magnificent home, Olive frequently found herself caught off guard by the fact this had happened to *her*. She would have to sit until the giddiness wore off. Other times she feared she was dreaming and would wake up any minute. But it wasn't a dream, and a twelve-room mansion was hers. *Her home.* Those two words sent a tingle down her spine. Having a place that belonged to her, even if she didn't have anyone to share it with, was a dream come true. After all, she'd spent a portion of her childhood in foster care. In her teen years, everything she'd owned could have fit in just a garbage bag. And, truth be told, she didn't have a ton of personal possessions now, but finally having a permanent place to call home was wonderful. Having a family of her own one day to fill that very home would be—

"Olive?"

The sound of Cal's voice brought her out of her thoughts. "Sorry. No. Reopening the B and B wasn't a requirement for entries, although I do have to live in the home myself, but that's not a hardship. I love the place. It has a few eccentricities but I'm learning to love those, too."

"So you can't unload the house?" His eyebrows dipped toward the bridge of his nose.

"Why would I want to?" she snapped. "I may not have grown up with the desire to run a B and B, but the idea has its appeal." She'd fallen into her current profession when her last foster mother had suffered a stroke and been placed in a skilled nursing facility. Olive had visited her often and become friendly with the other residents.

Prior to that, Olive had been uncertain about her

career path but looked into elder care and earned a bachelor's in health-care management with a certificate in senior-living management. During college she'd volunteered at the skilled nursing facility. Soon after graduation, the position of assistant activity director opened up at a large facility, where she gained enough experience to apply for an opening at the same place as her foster mother. Several years after accepting the job, her foster mother suffered another stroke and passed away, or Olive would never have considered leaving that facility.

She'd started researching what went into running a B and B when winning the place had been just a pie-in-the-sky dream for her. She might not have a family to call her own yet—or have had one growing up—but filling her house with other happy people and their children would go a long way toward filling that need in her, she knew. But it was as if fate had stepped in and given her a push. With her foster mother gone and her engagement broken, it had been easier to cut her ties to Worcester, Massachusetts. And the opening at Sunshine Gardens had been that final piece falling into place.

"Living there is one thing, but trying to open a B and B is going to be difficult. Do you have any idea the enormity of the undertaking?"

She stiffened at his dubious tone. In the past, she'd surpassed people's expectations of her. Her first foster parents had taken her shyness as a sign of low

intelligence and the other kids in the home had be-
rated her. And some of her teachers had scolded her
for a lack of ambition because she held herself apart,
preferring to assess a situation before jumping in.
As an adult, she'd learned that she required thinking
time before jumping into a task. It wasn't a lack of
anything, but simply the way her brain was wired.
If she'd listened to them, she wouldn't have earned a
college degree. Or found work in a field she enjoyed.
"Nothing worthwhile is ever easy."

"Not easy doesn't even begin to cover it. I haven't
been inside, but I shudder to think of all those violations." He shook his head and laughed.

The deep baritone of his laughter skittered across
her nerve endings and her stomach tensed. *Oh, my.*
She really would need to be cautious to keep her feelings reined in around him. It took a moment, because
she'd been distracted by his laugh and her reaction
to it, but his comment finally sunk in. "What do you
mean by violations?"

"Fire-code violations. I could give you a list off
the top of my head if you'd like."

Now the laughter balled in her stomach for a totally different reason. Talk about an about-face. Who
was he to be making fun of her aspirations, even if
she did have a lot to learn? Most of her energy had
been used to relocate and get accustomed to the routine at her new place of employment. Once settled,
she'd planned on putting time into researching every-

thing involving opening a B and B, including bringing things up to code. "That won't be necessary, but thank you, anyway."

She mentally kicked herself for even broaching the subject with him. Of course, she knew getting a business like a bed-and-breakfast off the ground wouldn't be exactly easy. She'd been in the house barely a month but already had a notebook full of wish lists and a laptop with bulging Pinterest pages. Having done some preliminary research into local contractors, licenses she'd need to obtain and regulations she'd need to abide by, Olive was aware she had a long way to go before she could declare her B and B open to the public. But she could picture the finished product and that vision fueled her determination to make it happen. Were this man's insinuations that she might fail his way of trying to be friendly? If so, he could learn a thing or two from Ellie about how to be kind to strangers.

She smiled at him, determined to remain friendly despite his skeptical attitude. "I know I have a lot of work ahead of me."

He scowled at her. "Did you think you could just take possession of the place and reopen?"

"Of course not. I'm not naive, Mr. Pope." *Didn't your former fiancé have a different opinion?* She pushed aside any thoughts of Kurt and straightened her shoulders. "Look, I—"

"Hey, you two." Liam tutted and pointed at them

both. "Cal, first day on the job and you're already harassing the town's newest resident?"

Olive blinked and glanced around, feeling a sudden heat scorch her cheeks. Everyone at the table was looking at them both and grinning. Great. Her first shot at making friends in her new town and she'd already gotten into an argument with the guest of honor. Would they ever invite her to join them again, or would they promptly cross her off the list? She could imagine everyone gossiping about them already.

She wanted to regret arguing with him. She *should* regret it. But she didn't. It wasn't so much Cal Pope's words that had had her blood pressure spiking; it was the manner in which those words were delivered. He'd laughed at her. At her plans. As if her feelings hadn't mattered. She'd spent too much of her childhood realizing that her feelings didn't matter once she was in the system.

Although it had been tough, she'd liked her first placement. So, after three months, when she'd been informed it was time to leave, she'd begged to stay. Both the caseworker and her foster parents explained that this had been short-term. Her foster mother informed her that they were what was considered emergency placement.

She could still remember asking why she couldn't stay and being told she needed to leave to free up a spot so her foster mother could take in another child.

At the time, the experience had made her feel as if she'd been shouting into the void.

As an adult she understood her removal hadn't been her fault and another person needed help, but she still hated to think that protocols could be more important than people.

She wasn't going to put up with it now, either, so she deliberately turned her back on Cal Pope and asked Mary Wilson how she could become involved in her summer camp for foster children.

Despite having turned her attention to Mary while talking with her, Olive was still acutely aware of the presence of the man seated next to her. She might have done her best to tune him out, but she had difficulty ignoring her physical reaction to his dark good looks. Besides, his remarks about her plans still irked her.

"So, tell me what it's like to live in such a grand house?" Mary asked, drawing Olive from her thoughts. "Do you get lost in all those rooms?"

"I had to buy some scatter rugs to cut down on the echo in the rooms that are sparsely furnished so far." Olive laughed. "Which is most of them."

Mary nodded. "Sadie's great-nephew probably took everything that wasn't nailed down. That house could use a bunch of kids running in the halls and playing in the yard."

"That's my fondest wish," Olive said and winced at the wistfulness she detected in her tone. She didn't need to spill her guts to people she'd just met. Hoping to lighten things up, she laughed. "I probably should find a husband first."

Mary smiled and leaned forward to look around Olive. "Hey, Cal, you still a confirmed bachelor?" Olive's heart dropped and she looked anywhere but at the firefighter at her side.

"Why? Are you finally planning on leaving Brody to run off with me?" Cal joked.

"What's this about my Mary running off?" Brody turned and gave Cal a narrowed-eye glare.

"Just as rumor." Mary patted her husband's hand. "Don't pay any attention."

Although Olive was enjoying getting to know Ellie's circle, she knew it would probably be best for all concerned to limit her interactions with Cal in the future. She was determined to make friends in Loon Lake, not lose them. If that meant staying clear of any arguments—or especially any romantic entanglements—with Cal, then so be it. She was in control of her libido. So for now she'd be polite and smile, even if she didn't feel like it.

Cal scowled at the back of Olive's head. He itched to twirl one of those curls around his finger. Would it be as soft as it appeared? Would it spring back once released?

What was wrong with him? He was thirty-five years old not some randy teen without any urge control. But that damn smile of hers was messing with his libido. Why her? What was it about Olive and her smile that made him act like such an ass? The waitress kept smiling at him, sending out signals, and it did nothing for him. Of course, that woman was most likely a college student and he was well past the age when coeds had caught his eye.

It wasn't as if Olive had any stake in her reopening the B and B or not. No, his rudeness was a direct result of that high-wattage, full-faced grin she kept aiming at him. *Bull's-eye.* It hit its mark each and every time, but his reaction was all out of proportion to the situation. Or was it? He hated to think of what could happen to her if there was ever a fire in that ramshackle building and she couldn't get out. That's what he should have told her, rather than jumping all over her and embarrassing her.

Olive laughed at something Mary said and that husky laugh curled around his belly. He tried to focus his attention on the waitress as she went around the table taking everyone's orders. Yeah, way too young for him. And she didn't have long, blond, corkscrew hair or that full-wattage smile.

His gaze moved back to his new neighbor. She shook her head at something Mary was saying, making her hair swish around her shoulders like a hula dancer's grass skirt. Even from the back, those blond curls fascinated him. No, *blond* was too bland a word to describe that color. There were shades of honey, amber and sun-kissed wheat.

Damn, but that wasn't helping. He glanced down the table, past Olive. He'd focus on the others at the table. Liam was his best friend and Ellie was like a sister to him. Ellie had told him how much she liked Olive, though, so hitting on her new coworker with no intention to making it permanent would be like making time with your sister's best friend, or your best friend's sister. A no-no in anyone's book. A double no-no in this case.

Except Riley and Liam were best buddies and Riley was now happily married to Liam's sister, Meg. *So it can happen*, a sly voice reminded him until he pushed it out of his head.

And something told him that Olive had "white picket fence" written all over her. And no way was he falling into that trap. Marriage and happily-ever-after were a myth. His own past was all the proof he needed.

But that didn't excuse him from scoffing at her plans for reopening the B and B. Even if everything he'd told her was true—he had a feeling that place was one code violation after another—he could have gotten his point across without being so rude. And he *had* upset her, but every time she turned that bright smile on him, it set off all sorts of warning bells in his head, unleashed all sorts of jitters in his gut and shaved points off his IQ.

The only other time he'd reacted on a gut level to a woman, she'd turned out to be an investigative journalist looking for a where-are-they-now? story about his father's financial crimes. Despite the ten-year statute of limitations running out, whenever a similar crime happened, his father's notorious actions were once again dragged out for public consumption. Embezzling millions and never getting caught turned the ugly business into a myth similar to the state's infamous unsolved Berkshire armored-car robbery in Rutland.

Mary was temporarily diverted as the waitress took her order. In that interval, Cal used the distraction to touch Olive's arm to gain her attention.

She turned toward him, a slight furrow marring her brow. "Something wrong?"

He did his best to ignore the urge to explore that little wrinkle with his hands and his lips, and pasted on a smile, hoping the expression didn't look as pained as it felt. "I owe you an apology."

"Oh," she said and blinked.

"I shouldn't have jumped on you about code violations."

She shrugged. "It is your job, and you take it seriously."

"I do, but that's not an excuse to be rude. I'm your neighbor," he added, "and you might not have known that stuff." *Besides, you're far too beautiful to have your brow furrowed like that...* He dismissed those intrusive thoughts with a concerted effort.

Olive nodded and half smiled at him in acknowledgment, then turned back to Mary to resume their conversation. Though she'd apparently accepted his apology, Cal found himself feeling strangely unsatisfied.

What did you want? he asked himself sarcastically. *Her to jump into your arms and start kissing you passionately?* The idea appealed to him more than he wanted to admit, and he began talking to his friends.

The rest of dinner passed swiftly, with Cal sneaking covert glances at Olive. They didn't speak further at the meal, but he wondered what she was thinking. *She's definitely not thinking about* you, he told himself forcefully. *Definitely. Not.*

These ruminations continued as the friends exited to the parking lot and split off to drive home.

Shaking his head at his thoughts, he started the engine and pulled out of the parking spot. He drove along Main Street, passing the town green, with its restored white gazebo that doubled as a bandstand for concerts and picnics in the summer. He passed the brick-fronted businesses and the white Greek Revival church, with its black shutters and steeple bell tower. These gave way to rectangular early nineteenth-century gable-roofed houses, some of which had been repurposed into doctors' and attorneys' offices.

He'd enjoyed his time in the air force but something about Loon Lake had called to him. As a result, he'd returned to his hometown to work in the fire department, despite the difficult memories from his childhood. But that wasn't strictly true, as not all of his memories were bad. There were a lot of good ones, too. Of course, his father's actions the summer Cal had turned fifteen eclipsed any good for many years. Cal felt that returning to the scene of his dad's crime, as it were, had been the right thing. Some of those good memories were returning, helping to replace the bad, and he was making new ones.

He pushed aside those thoughts. Thinking about the past was unproductive. Slowing, he turned onto his street. As usual, the majestic Queen Anne Victorian, now a fairy-tale castle-shaped hulk in the darkness, captured his attention. The once-beautiful home had fascinated him as a child and, despite it falling into disrepair in the past decade, that fascination hadn't waned. And now, having met the current owner, he was even more curious.

He hadn't had a chance to really get to know the previous owner, Sadie. He'd talked to her several times in passing after he'd moved into his place, and she'd mentioned the conditions of her will. He would've sworn he didn't have a romantic bone in his body, but he understood Sadie's attachment to the home. And Olive's, too. He might have understood Sadie's attachment, but he still considered the contest business a bad idea. Look at how it was tying Olive into knots trying to take care of the place. The nature of the contest almost guaranteed the home would end up in the hands of someone unprepared to take on such a project.

Darkness shrouded many of the house's features, but he knew them by heart and could picture the home in his mind. The well-proportioned structural components included elaborate dormers and gables, plus a three-story octagonal tower. The gingerbread trim was ornate and plentiful, but not too ostentatious. In his opinion, the crowning glory was the porch, which ran the length of the front and curved around the tower on the side.

"Veranda," he corrected himself. That old-fashioned term was the only way to describe the grand porch.

He pulled into his driveway and turned off the engine. Enough thinking about the house, and Olive, its new occupant, for one night. He'd do his best to avoid her—and that smile that was so charming it could make him consider buying swampland in Florida—in the future.

Despite his resolve, he couldn't help glancing across the street as he shut the door of his truck.

She'd come onto the porch and was silhouetted in the light cast from the house through the open front door. Was that a watering can in her hand? He shook his head. If she wanted to water plants at ten in the evening, that was her business. He wasn't—

A sudden squeal and a crash stopped him in his tracks, and he whirled around. Olive was still on her porch, but was frantically flailing her arms about.

The sight spurred him into action, and he sprinted across the street to her, his heart pounding hard enough to escape his chest. Once there, he leaped up the steps, nearly tripping on the watering can, which was lying, abandoned, on the veranda's wooden floor. After kicking it aside, he reached out and grabbed her by the elbows. "Olive? What is it? What's wrong?"

She was practically hyperventilating. He looked around, trying to find the source of her distress, and found nothing.

He gently pushed her into one of the wicker chairs and hunkered down in front of her. "Put your head between your legs."

She opened her mouth, but nothing came out.

"Between your legs," he said again.

Shaking her head, she said, "I'm fine now. Honest."

He studied her face. She was pale but her breathing had slowed; she seemed to have recovered. "Wanna tell me what happened?"

"Not really." She huffed out a small laugh. "But I guess you deserve an explanation." She inhaled. "I—I was going to water the hanging ferns. I meant to do it this morning before work and forgot. I did the first and—" she took a shuddering breath "—I walked into a humongous spiderweb. I didn't see it in the dark."

"A spider's web?" She'd practically given him a heart attack over a stupid spiderweb? He'd rescued soldiers in the midst of battle, dodging incoming rounds as he accompanied the wounded to the helicopters waiting to extricate them from combat. Not once had he reacted as he had when he heard Olive's cry. Was he going soft or was this particular woman getting to him already?

"You walked into a spiderweb?" Relief made his tone curt.

"Yes, I walked into a spiderweb," she repeated, sarcasm dripping from her voice. "I realize that is nothing compared to what you must've seen or experienced during your time in Afghanistan or even as a firefighter once you came home."

She pulled away from his grip on her elbows and he dropped his arms to his side. He hadn't even realized he'd still been holding on to her. He rose and took a step back.

"I'm sorry if I startled you."

Startled him? *Lady, you have no idea.* He swallowed the harsh words that bubbled up. Once again, his reaction to her was his fault, not hers.

"You scared me," he admitted. "I thought you might be seriously hurt or in danger. That really got to me." *Just pour your heart out, why don't ya? Get a grip*, he ordered himself.

"I really am sorry," she said in a small voice and glanced down at her feet.

Now he felt like a heel. What was it about this woman that had him tied in knots every time he interacted with her? "I'm just glad you're okay."

"I'm fine." She nodded, then smiled. "Well, except for those nightmares I'm going to have about spiders getting stuck in my hair."

"Are you an arachnophobe?"

"I prefer to call it a healthy respect for insects and creepy-crawlies. They can live their lives as long as they let me live mine. Preferably without our paths crossing."

"Good philosophy." He let out a rough chuckle. "I feel that way about clowns. And, yeah, I know ninety-three percent of the population treat it as a joke."

"I guess I'm one of that percentage that doesn't get it, but I can respect it."

"Thanks." He glanced around. "And if that gets out, I'll know the source."

"I assure you—they won't hear it from me," she said and crossed her heart. "And thank you—again—for coming to my rescue."

"Even if you didn't really need it?"

"Especially then," she said. When he raised an

eyebrow, she continued, "I mean, I wasn't exactly pleasant toward you tonight at dinner."

He waved off her words with one hand. "I was the one who was rude, not you. I shouldn't have laughed."

"No, you shouldn't have."

"And I'm sorry for that."

"Well, it's your job to know all those things about fire safety and code violations. And I would expect you to be zealous about it. I hope when the time comes, I can count on your guidance."

"I'll be here for you."

Wait...what? I'll be here? he thought, admonishing himself as he stood up to go home. *No. You're going to stay away from Olive Downing. Far, far away.*

Chapter Two

Olive stirred the macaroni salad she'd mixed up last night, letting the flavors blend as the recipe suggested. Sunshine Gardens's business office manager had just returned from vacation in Hawaii and was raving about the islands and the food. Olive figured this dish might be as close as she'd get to a Hawaiian vacation, so she made some after searching the internet for what promised to be an authentic recipe.

The ingredients and the recipe might have been simple but buying them had been an adventure. Instead of going to Pic-N-Save, the town's grocery store, Olive had elected to go to Loon Lake General Store, since it was owned by a resident, and she believed in supporting local businesses.

She smiled to herself as she dished out a small portion for a taste test. Ellie had told her the owner, Octavia "Tavie" Whatley, was a character. Olive now understood that was code for "busybody." The woman seemed to know everyone and everything about the town.

Tavie had scolded her for not coming in sooner. Not because she wanted her business, but because she'd wanted Olive to satisfy her curiosity about the contest. Olive had answered her questions, knowing that what she said would soon be fodder for the gossip mill. Olive knew that was part of small-town life and accepted it. This was her new hometown and she wanted to fit it even if it meant revealing something about herself.

Satisfied the mac salad was tasty, she resealed the plastic container with its lid. She glanced at the analog-style schoolhouse clock on the wall above her small maple kitchen dining set.

Time to make a decision.

She went to stand behind the sheer white curtains at the picture window in the front parlor. She chuckled at her use of that designation for this portion of her house. It wasn't as if she had a back one. Cal was the reason she was standing here, spying on the neighbor. If she wasn't careful, she'd turn into one of those curtain twitchers. Like the foster mother in her second placement. The woman had appointed herself the neighborhood monitor. She gossiped so much about the neighbors, Olive often wondered what she'd told them about her. A few of the neighborhood children had taunted her, saying she had to live with strangers because no one else had wanted her. She'd cried and asked her foster mother if she was a burden. The woman had told her she wasn't because she was compensated by the state. When she'd relayed this to the other children, one explained that people were getting paid to take care of her. After that she was careful what she said to anyone.

A week had passed since the embarrassing spiderweb incident on the porch, and she had avoided prolonged one-on-one contact with Cal when they were in a group with mutual friends. A nod here or there, and that was about it. But she kept her eye on him as often as she could. She couldn't seem to help herself.

Movement caught her attention as Cal emerged from his house. He glanced across the street toward her, and she took an automatic step back.

"Talk about regressing to adolescence, spying on the cute guy across the street," she muttered, shaking her head at her behavior.

Kurt, her ex, had been the one who'd instigated their first meeting. She'd been supplementing her income with a part-time job as a barista at the local coffee chain to help pay off her student-loan debt. She'd had a crush on the cute guy who stopped in every morning and flirted with her as he ordered a two-shot latte. He'd called her cute while she'd blushed and stammered. She sighed and pushed out those thoughts. No need to live in the past. She was building a new life for herself in the present.

She'd been invited to a joint cookout between the McBrides and the Coopers today. Did she want to go, considering Cal would be there and their previous interactions had been what could only be thought of as embarrassing? She straightened her shoulders. She wasn't a coward, though. Maybe Cal would bring a date to the picnic. Yeah, that would be a good thing, because then she'd be able to forget her attraction to him, the man who'd insulted her and then apologized and had come to her rescue from a "threat." She could finally stop this what-if nonsense every time she thought about him or saw him coming or going from his house, wondering if he had a girlfriend, or what he looked for in a woman. She could stop her childish mooning over her gorgeous neighbor.

Why was she even questioning if she *should* go? Olive was new to town and wanted to connect with her fellow Loon Lake residents. She'd see him today at the picnic, and they'd laugh over her walking into the spiderweb and that would be that. She grabbed her keys and the macaroni salad she'd made, then left the house.

After a short drive, she pulled her Camry into the long driveway shared by two families. The two homes were surrounded on three sides by trees, making it seem as if they were the only signs of life in the wilderness. Olive had learned that these had started out as modest summer cottages, but both had been expanded and turned into year-round family houses that shared not only a driveway, but also large front yards that abutted one another.

Riley and Meg Cooper lived in one with their three children, Fiona, James and Timothy. Liam and Ellie lived in the other with their two-year-old twins, Sean and Bridget. Ellie had told her how the arrangement fostered a close relationship between her twins and their cousins. Olive hoped that if she had children of her own someday that she could give them deep roots like that. She might not have blood relatives, but if she had a few close friends like Ellie, Meg and Mary, her kids could be close to theirs.

Olive couldn't prevent herself from glancing around at everyone gathered in the shared yard. She recognized Cal's truck and parked behind it. Ellie was headed toward the house, but veered toward Olive instead. Ellie was dressed casually in shorts and a T-shirt with her long dark hair pulled back into her usual efficient ponytail.

Olive decided to leave her purse in the car but grabbed the plastic container she'd set on the floor of the passenger side.

"Sorry if I'm a bit late, looks like everyone is here already," Olive said as she scooted out. She'd been the last one to arrive at Hennen's that night, too. In the past, she would have called herself a punctual person. So what was so different now? She certainly didn't do it so she could make an entrance. Quite the opposite. Would that make her too noticeable, but not in a good way?

"You're not late. Mary and Brody aren't here yet." Ellie looked at the bowl of macaroni salad. "Ooh, is this your famous Hawaiian mac salad you brought to work for that picnic?"

Olive laughed. "I'm not sure about famous but it's that mac salad I made for the gathering we had at work. I made it because it's my favorite but the recipe yields way too much for a single person."

"Lucky for us." Ellie leaned closer as they walked toward where the others were gathered. "Cal arrived about ten minutes ago. He came solo, in case you were wondering."

"Oh, I wasn't..."

Yeah, she was, and she spotted him standing next to Riley Cooper. Both men stood sipping beer from green, longneck bottles. Of similar height, they also had the same body type—fit but not muscle-bound. Olive smiled at their contrasting hairstyles. Riley kept his neat and closely cropped, possibly due to his job as sheriff's deputy, and Cal's longer hair was unkempt as usual. But the most striking difference was that while Riley Cooper was a fine, handsome man, he didn't make her heart drum faster when she was looking at him. Even dressed as he was in casual clothing, just cargo shorts and a T-shirt, Cal set off a swarm of butterflies in her stomach. Cal was gesturing with his free hand and Riley was nodding. Talking shop, or sports?

"Uh-huh," Ellie murmured. "Why didn't you two come to the cookout together? You could have carpooled."

Ellie's question broke into her thoughts and Olive felt warmth rise to face. Did her new friend suspect that her feelings for Cal already went beyond neighborly? She hoped not, because she didn't need anyone trying to play matchmaker, especially with the gruff but handsome firefighter just across the street. Sure, if Cal wanted the same things she did, she might be tempted, but from what she'd heard, he didn't. Several of the nursing assistants at Sunshine Gardens had spoken fondly of him but also said he wasn't into commitment. One had graduated high school with him, another had been on a date with him after his return from the air force and one said her husband was also a firefighter and knew Cal professionally.

During her visit to Loon Lake General Store, Tavie verified Cal was considered a "catch" by some of the single ladies in town. According to Tavie, a cashier at the Pic-N-Save had dated him, but as soon as she hinted at her desire for more, he broke it off.

A warning if she'd ever heard one. Why start something she knew was doomed to fail? After what happened with Kurt, she wasn't sure her heart could take another beating. And the funny thing was, now that she looked back on it, losing Kurt didn't hurt as much in the long run as losing his family and their shared friends. She refused to open herself up to such pain again. When she fell in love once more, she vowed that it would be forever.

Olive reluctantly tore her gaze away from Cal. "Were we supposed to come together?"

"No. But why wouldn't you?" Ellie made a clucking sound with her tongue. "You live across the street from one another."

"True, but our paths didn't cross this week to co-ordinate anything." Olive's gaze once again tracked Cal as he and Riley strolled over to the kids playing soccer. Riley's oldest, Fiona, was trying to corral the younger ones into something that resembled a true game, but they were having too much fun just running in all directions and chasing the ball. She wondered if she'd ever have a family like that, with kids scattered around her front lawn, and felt her heart ache at the thought. "And with his job and all, I understand he can get called in at a moment's notice to investigate suspicious fires."

"I know you came here from a city like Worcester in Massachusetts, but you've been in Loon Lake long enough to realize that's not likely to happen. And, if by some chance it did, you could walk home. After all, it's only six-point-two miles."

"I know, but…did you just say you'd make me walk home?"

Ellie laughed. "So, you were listening. The way you were checking out Cal, I wasn't so sure."

"I wasn't checking him out." Her denial sounded hollow even to her own ears. Sure, she'd been physically attracted to Kurt when he'd come into the coffee shop, but she was older, more experienced now, and what she'd felt for Kurt back then hadn't gone this deep until she'd gotten to know him. As she thought back, she knew her feelings for her ex must have grown because she'd agreed to spend her life with him, but now she had trouble trying to remember. Had she done that good of a job at burying the past, or had her longing for a family of her own—and Kurt had a big one—prompted her to say yes?

"Then you must have been checking out my brother-in-law? Sorry, Olive, but Riley is spoken for. He and Meg are not only in love, but procreating at a steady rate."

"I wasn't checking out Riley," she insisted. "I know he and Meg are— You're doing it again. I'm listening to you." Olive shook her head, but the truth was, she had been busy checking out Cal. "And there's nothing sickening about being in love with your spouse. And you're one to talk. You and Liam are a wonderful example of wedded bliss."

Olive could only hope for a relationship like Ellie and Liam had, or Meg and Riley. Her parents had died when she was eleven, but she thought she remembered them holding hands, her dad telling her that she and her mom were the loves of his life. Or was she just projecting? As one foster sibling had pointed out, they'd died without leaving provisions for the care of their only child.

Ellie glanced over at her husband, who was lighting the barbecue grill. As if sensing his wife's gaze, he looked up and zeroed in on her. His look of pure love and adoration said it all.

"Want me to give you guys some privacy?" Olive playfully bumped her friend's shoulder with hers.

Ellie laughed. "I can't help it if I want you to find what I have."

"I'm sure I will someday." She still had plenty of time to start a family. At least that's what she'd told herself on her most recent birthday. But she still had to find the right man, someone who would believe in her and be faithful. Who knew when that might happen?

Ellie glanced around. "I have a confession to make."

"Oh?" Did her friend regret throwing her in Cal's path? Had Cal told her he wasn't interested in her that way? She could only speculate about her handsome neighbor.

"When I invited you to join us at Hennen's, I was hoping that maybe—" she shrugged "—maybe you and Cal would hit it off. Liam said I shouldn't have done that, though."

Olive debated over asking Ellie why Cal didn't want a committed relationship. Something might have happened in his past to cause his attitude. She might want answers, but she didn't want to overstep. After all, her and Ellie's friendship was still new and she didn't want to make her new pal uncomfortable talking about Cal behind his back.

"We weren't really arguing, even if it might have seemed like it," Olive assured her. "At least not angrily. And he apologized afterward for being a bit rude."

"Oh, I know that." Ellie waved her hand as if shooing away a fly. "I meant that Liam got after me later when he suspected I'd been trying to matchmake. I'm sorry if I made things uncomfortable."

Olive didn't want her pal, and she now considered Ellie one, to regret including her in any social activity. "You didn't. Cal is a really nice guy."

"Yeah, but as Liam likes to point out, he's also a commitmentphobe."

"That's okay, since I'm an arachnophobe," Olive murmured, remembering the incident.

"What?" Ellie turned her head toward her and frowned.

Olive laughed. "Nothing. Just a little inside joke."

For some inexplicable reason she didn't want to share the little moment she and Cal had had. It was probably dangerous to even think like that, but that moment had felt intimate, like something shared just between the two of them. Even if it was just her neighbor helping calm her down after she'd seen a giant spider. *His gentle manner then really was something*, she thought to herself.

"You'll find someone," Ellie said.

"I'm sure I will." But that someone wouldn't be Cal Pope. She wasn't inherently against a little no-strings-attached fun, but at this stage in her life, she wanted more, something permanent. And she hoped it happened while she could still have time to get started on a family.

"Oh, dear, looks like I have to rescue Sean from his sister," Ellie said as a squabble broke out between the McBride twins.

"Go. I'll pop this into your refrigerator until we're ready for it." Olive lifted her bowl of mac salad as her heart thumped in her chest. She wanted what Ellie and Liam had one day—a loving relationship, and kids. But for that, she'd have to find a man who wanted the same things—unlike Kurt. Or Cal, for that matter. Not that she was thinking of him in that way...

Could she even trust her judgment? Kurt had told her a lot of things, promised a lot of things...but they'd all been lies. His father was grooming him to take over the family business but had wanted his son to be settled, married. Kurt had wanted to have his cake and eat it, too, and had obviously thought her naive enough not to ask too many questions. He'd thought because of her background she'd be grateful and not question him as she had.

"Thanks. You should be able to squeeze it onto one of the shelves. As long as you're going in, could you do me a favor and get the kids' sunscreen? I left it on the counter in the bathroom in the hall outside the twins' bedroom."

"Sure, no problem." Olive had been to Ellie and Liam's place a few times before, so she was familiar with the interior.

After finding a spot for the salad in the crowded refrigerator, Olive ducked down the hall to get the sunscreen.

As she picked up the bottle, the back door creaked open, and voices drifted to her from the kitchen, so she stopped for a moment.

Someone groaned. "Not you, too."

"Whaddaya mean?" another person said.

"She's like a spider spinning a web. Waiting to trap an unsuspecting man."

"What the hell are you…? Here, hold this for me and don't drink it. My sister grabbed my last one and it was practically empty by the time I wrestled it away from her."

There was a noise like cardboard being ripped open. "What's this nonsense about a trap?" the second voice asked.

"I heard Olive Downing is looking for a husband. Wants to fill that house with kids." Embarrassment flooded her body; her cheeks grew hot as she wished the ground could just swallow her up. *That voice is probably Cal's*, she realized, feeling humiliated.

"So? What's wrong with that? If I wasn't madly in love with my wife, I'd..."

She stayed out of sight in the hallway. Eavesdropping was wrong but she couldn't force her feet to work. The other voice sounded like Liam.

"She's got that house, so now she's on the hunt for a husband to go with it. Complete the picture," Cal said. Olive grew irritated; he barely even knew her. How dare he assume what she wanted out of life after knowing her only a week! He was the worst kind of person—the type who made assumptions based on just a handful of words exchanged.

"Cut her some slack. You make her sound like some sort of man-eating shark. She's not like that. She's sweet," Liam said.

"She's—"

"Hey, where's those beers?" Another voice broke in. "You guys taking your time to brew them or what?"

"Yeah. Yeah. Hold your horses, we're coming."

She heard the clanking of bottles, then the screen door opening and slamming shut. Olive leaned back against the wall. She pressed her hand to her stomach, which felt like it was in free fall after hearing that conversation. She hadn't hidden the fact she longed for a family of her own, but was that so bad? He'd made it sound like she was some sort of predator... waiting to trap some unsuspecting victim. Like that spider on her porch. *And I'm not desperate for any man, let alone you, Cal Pope!* she thought defiantly.

She pulled away from the wall, trying to control her breathing. She headed back to the bathroom and quietly shut the door, even though she knew she was now alone in the house. If she gave in and slammed the door, she might not be able to hold everything together. She sat on the closed toilet lid.

Clenching her hands in her lap, she took several deep breaths.

She'd have to watch herself around Cal. When Kurt had broken off their engagement, she hadn't just lost a fiancé, but also his family, who were like her own, and friends. Kurt had taken them all with him when he'd left, and they'd seemingly gone willingly. It was probably a good thing they hadn't married because she now realized she missed the people around Kurt more than she did Kurt himself. But one thing was for sure—she wasn't going through that type of heartbreak again. Not for any man...and definitely not for Cal Pope.

She stood up, then ran the water and washed her hands, checked her face and went back to the cookout.

Once outside again, Olive watched as Cal pretended to get tackled by Mary's son, Elliott, and then

Ellie's son, Sean, joined the fun and hopped on. Cal looked as if he was enjoying rolling around on the grass as much as the two boys. Watching scenes like this, it was hard to believe Cal was against marriage and fatherhood.

Maybe he just doesn't want any of that with you, an insidious voice taunted her. She wasn't so egotistical as to think guys couldn't resist her. Absolutely not. Just look at Kurt and their broken engagement. Despite feeling—deep, deep down—a bit relieved when he'd wanted to call off the wedding. Had she known in the darkest part of her heart that she'd been willing to settle? Kurt hadn't set off any fireworks and she'd thought maybe she wasn't the type to feel that kind of attraction, and maybe she didn't set them off in anyone else. At first, Kurt had seemed like he was a nice guy and she had pictured a future with him. Had she been selling herself short?

But maybe the way things had ended was for the best. Because if she was being brutally honest with herself, Kurt hadn't made her tummy roll the way Cal did. Falling for the wrong guy again was not in her plans. She didn't consider herself a prude, but she'd never been the type for casual relationships. Besides, she couldn't imagine having sex with someone without involving her emotions. And if her emotions were involved, it would be difficult seeing him casually after the sex ended. Even if she could engage in a strictly physical exchange. She knew it would break her heart to become involved with someone and then continue to see him after it ended. Today, for example. How would she feel if he'd brought another woman to the picnic?

She was already feeling close to this group of friends and knew she'd miss them terribly if she had to give them up. It might be easier in the long run to give up exploring her physical reaction to Cal instead of her friendships. Of course, that still meant taking care to guard her heart.

"Hey, why so glum? This is a party." Meg Cooper flopped down on a chair and nudged her knee against Olive's. "What gives?"

Olive plastered a smile on her face for Liam's sister. "Nothing. I'm having a great time and I really appreciate the invitation."

"Sure thing," Meg said and took a sip of the beer in her hand.

"You have a lovely home. It must be nice to live so close to family." Any biological family she might have had were not close, or into welcoming her into their families. Some distant cousins of her parents had been willing to dispose of their belongings, but not willing to take responsibility for a child. And the one foster sister she'd been close to had joined the military, and they hadn't done more than exchange Christmas cards the last few years.

Meg laughed. "It has its moments, but I love Ellie, so I put up with having my brother so close."

Olive joined her and laughed but her gaze sought out Cal as he played with the kids.

Meg's gaze followed Olive's and she made a sound in her throat. "Ah. I see what was putting that frown on your face."

"What? There's nothing to see." Olive knew her face must be red and hated that she couldn't control the heat that rose and must now be coloring her fair skin.

"Uh-huh. Cal's a nice guy but I think what happened when he was younger screwed him up and made him commitment-averse."

"And a leopard doesn't change its spots." *But why is he commitment-averse?* she wondered. She wanted desperately to pry into Cal's past, to ask Meg what the local scuttlebutt about his youth was, but she was afraid she'd look too interested and give herself away.

"I wouldn't give up hope," Meg said. "It may look like all happy families here—and don't get me wrong, because we are—but not everyone here had an easy time getting to that point."

Olive knew a bit about Meg's own history. How the man who was now her husband had left for combat without knowing Meg was pregnant with their daughter. But luckily, they'd worked out their problems when Riley had returned to Loon Lake. He and Meg were now happily married and the proud parents of three children.

"Does he date much?" she asked Meg.

"Well, he's no serial dater, but, yeah, I'd say he has dated."

Again, Olive's thoughts turned to the fact that maybe Cal just wasn't interested in anything serious or permanent with *her*. "I'm not counting on being the one to get him to change."

"I wouldn't be too sure about that. I've seen the way he looks at you."

"What? How?"

Meg chuckled. "Like he wants to eat you up."

Olive shook her head fiercely. "No. If anything, he probably wants to educate me on fire codes."

"Hey, it's a starting point."

Before Olive could respond, a big dog with a copper-colored curly coat galloped over, followed by a girl of around ten with the matching hair. Meg and Riley's daughter, Fiona—the girl was a miniature Meg. The dog sat but wriggled his entire body with excitement, so Olive reached out and stroked the dog's silky ears.

"And what's your name?" she asked the friendly dog.

"That's Mangy," Meg told her.

Olive quirked an eyebrow. "Mangy?"

"My daughter named him. Fiona, get over here and rescue our guest. She doesn't want him slobbering all over her," Meg called to her eldest, who was bouncing on her toes while standing next to some of the other kids.

"It's okay. I love animals. I used to have a cat, Max. I know cats don't have the same reputation for bonding with their owners. What's that saying? Dogs have owners, cats have staff. But that's not true—or wasn't for me. If you give a cat love and consideration, most times they will return the favor." She knew she'd eventually get another cat or maybe even a dog. When she pictured her future family, animals were always in the mix with kids.

"Oh, I'm sorry. Did you lose him?"

Olive nodded and swallowed. That wound was still fresh. Max had been with her since she'd aged out of the system at eighteen. So, all her adult life. He'd been her confidant and friend. Her comfort when her engagement ended. "Within days of moving here."

"That's too bad."

Olive sighed. "He was nineteen, so he had a good long life."

"Wow. You had him a long time."

"Yes, but not his whole life. I was eighteen and they estimated he was three or four."

"Still a long time. Fiona, get over here now."

The girl reluctantly got out of line and ran over.

"You were supposed to tie him up so he couldn't bother everyone."

"But it's gonna be my turn to play with Cal." The girl sent her curly hair bouncing around her shoulders. Olive wondered if she'd ever have a daughter of her own, a miniature version of her. She had an impression of her own dad saying how much she'd taken after her mom. But again, was that a real memory or one she'd made up as comfort?

"It'll only take a minute," Meg said.

"But, *Mom.*"

"But, Fiona," Meg replied, imitating her daughter as she gave her a look that parents had been perfecting for centuries. "Now."

As disparate as her foster mothers had been, they'd all shared that one look.

"Sorry about Mangy, Miss Olive."

"That's quite a name you gave him."

The girl rolled her eyes. "I was just a kid when I named him."

Olive bit the inside of her cheek. "I still like it."

"Uncle Liam says all the good names were taken."

Olive smiled. "That sounds like him."

"I get him back by calling him Leem. Remember, Mom, how I didn't used to be able to say his name right?" Fiona giggled and took the dog's collar. "C'mon, Mangy, you were supposed to behave yourself. You made me miss my turn with Cal."

The dog whined but went willingly with Fiona.

"I think my daughter has a crush on our fire marshal," Meg observed with a glance at Cal once Fiona was out of earshot.

"Do you blame her?" Olive said and immediately regretted it. She hadn't meant to say such a thing out loud. She didn't want to give anyone any encouragement. Not after what she'd overheard in the house and how Cal thought she was out to trap a man into being her husband.

She didn't know Meg as well as she did Ellie, but she liked her and felt they could become good friends, too. It was another reason she couldn't act on the chemistry between herself and Cal, if he was even so inclined. He might be able to explore the spark between them and move on once they had, but she wasn't made like that. She'd find it too hard to hang out with him and their friends, who might even decide to ditch her and pick Cal. Nor would she ever want to put them in a situation where they had to choose. No, she had stepped away. And damn it, she didn't want to step away from the friends she'd made since moving to Loon Lake. With no biological family of her own, her friends had always filled that void. And the last thing she'd want to do was endanger the new life she was slowly but surely building for herself, piece by piece, here in town.

Meg laughed and nudged Olive. "Don't worry. Your secret about Cal is safe with me. I'm Fort Knox."

"I only meant…" Olive sighed, wondering how she was going to get out of this.

"I don't blame you, you know. If I wasn't so stupidly in love with my husband, I'd be tempted." She laughed at the look Olive gave her. "I'm married, not dead."

"Well, you seem very happy together."

"Deliriously. I'll let you in on a little secret. When he proposed, and I accepted, we agreed to two or three more kids. Well, now he wants to try for one more, hoping to get another girl."

"And you don't want to try again?"

"Oh, I do, but I'd like the *trying* phase to last a bit longer, but judging by past experience I'll get pregnant right away. Liam thinks there's something in the water that's causing it."

"The water? Do you both have to drink it?" Olive laughed, despite the ache deep in her gut. What she wouldn't give to be in Meg's shoes. She didn't like to think of herself as a jealous person, but she did have to admit to being envious of her new friend's seemingly blissful life.

She glanced over at Cal playing badminton. *Bad move, Olive*. His closest friends knew him, and all agreed that he wasn't a guy to pin her future on. A couple of her coworkers had also voiced misgivings about Kurt. They'd hinted that she should ask him point-blank about their concerns. This time she would heed the warnings.

Cal heard Olive's laugh and let the shuttlecock fly right by him. He hadn't even raised his racket. Instead, he had immediately sought out the source of the sound like a heat-seeking missile. Glancing over, he found that she was sitting next to Meg and the two were engrossed in conversation.

"You playing? Or just going to gawk at your new neighbor all afternoon?" Liam asked him.

Cal told him what he could do with his racket.

"Ooh, did I hit a sore spot, Pope?"

Great. That's all he needed—everyone ragging on him about Olive. "Maybe I was looking at your sister."

Liam guffawed. "Nice try but I know she's safe."

"And why is that?"

"For one, she's so gaga in love with Riley it's sickening, and I know you don't poach. You might be a hound dog when it comes to women but only with available women."

"Your faith in me is heartening, McBride."

"Hey, you know I'm just pulling your chain."

"Yeah." Cal laughed. "My world is too small to become a serial dater."

Liam chuckled. "You could spend your free time in Boston or Burlington."

"Hey, I finally got the house finished. I want to enjoy it for a while."

"I get that, but what's wrong with Olive?" Liam asked.

"Nothing's wrong with her, but like I said, we're not wanting the same things out of life." He never should have said what he did, but his reaction to Olive was growing stronger and it spooked him. Still, that wasn't an excuse for crass behavior. He could only pray she never found out about that conversation.

"Hey, I wasn't sold on the whole marriage-and-kids thing, either, but it's the best thing that's ever happened to me."

Cal shook his head. Yeah, people always said that until the bottom dropped out of their world. Although he had to admit that he couldn't imagine either Liam or Ellie doing anything to cause harm to their partner. Not the way his dad had betrayed him and his mom.

His dad's story wasn't unique. Guys approaching a certain age often took up with younger women. Of course, not all disappeared with their clients' investment money, along with that younger woman. And not all the wives left behind checked out emotionally, as his mom had.

He often wondered if he just didn't pick up on the signals, or had his dad done such a good job of hiding his true nature? Or was it a simple midlife crisis with a little larceny thrown in? He hadn't suspected deception from that investigative journalist, either, so maybe he was just a lousy judge of character.

Something tugged at Olive's heart when she watched kids climb all over Cal. She blinked back tears at the domestic scene. This is what she'd always wanted for herself. And it was sad that a guy who obviously cared for children didn't want any of his own. She had trouble understanding the dichotomy of the situation. Did he just not want the responsibility?

"He'd make a super dad."

Olive startled. It was as if her thoughts had been given a voice. Ellie had sidled up to her while she'd been engrossed in Cal's byplay with Sean and Bridget.

"He's made it clear he's a confirmed bachelor," Olive said, as much for her own benefit as for Ellie.

Ellie gave her a look, speculation gleaming in her eyes. "Yeah, so was Liam."

Olive found that hard to believe. "What happened to change his mind?"

"I got pregnant with the twins," Ellie said in a matter-of-fact tone.

Olive turned to stare, wide-eyed, at her friend. She opened her mouth, but before anything came out, Ellie laughed and gave her a playful shoulder bump. "Don't look so shocked. The pregnancy wasn't on purpose, but I admit it was a welcome surprise."

Olive touched her friend's arm. "Because of the cancer?"

Everyone in Loon Lake knew Ellie was a childhood cancer survivor. Had she also struggled with fertility as an adult? Olive didn't know.

"Yeah, it was never a question of 'no, it won't happen' but more of a 'we doubt it will.' It's a blessing, although..." Ellie noticed her rambunctious twins playing and laughed. "It can sometimes be a bit questionable.

"Of course, our path wasn't without its blips, but Liam wanted to be there for us. We fell in love and we managed to work things out with our little family."

Ellie glanced across the yard, where Liam was flipping burgers on the grill with one hand and had a longneck bottle of pale ale dangling from the other. He lifted his head, and his gaze found his wife's and a goofy grin spread across his face. Olive's heart constricted at the obvious bond passing between the couple. That's what she longed for and realized with a painful jab that with Kurt she'd been willing to settle for comfortable.

She glanced over to Cal. Ellie had said she and Liam had had to work things out. Could she allow herself to— No! That path led to heartache. She wouldn't fall for the most unsuitable man she'd ever met—who just happened to be her irresistible neighbor.

Chapter Three

"I swear, Calvin Pope, if you were wound any tighter, you'd be a Timex." Tavie Whatley was standing behind the scarred, wood-topped counter and twirled a crooked, arthritic finger in his direction.

"You know better than to use extension cords." Cal pretended to study the clipboard in his hand, hoping to hide the grin he couldn't contain. Tavie spoke the truth, but he didn't want to encourage the septuagenarian owner of Loon Lake General Store. She might somehow divine the reason for his being tied in knots, wondering if Olive had somehow overheard his conversation with Liam. He regretted how he'd spoken about Olive, as if she was a man-eater intent on snaring her prey. He had just been feeling defensive, trying to resist his attraction to the newcomer, who he knew would be all wrong for him. And he couldn't let word of him liking Olive *that way* to leak out to Tavie. If she heard one word, the Loon Lake gossip mill would circulate, courtesy of the store owner.

His friend wouldn't have told Olive, but he might have told Ellie, who might have let it slip. Oh, man, this was getting complicated, and they hadn't even done anything! As a matter of fact, she appeared to be avoiding speaking with him in the week since the cookout. Or maybe they'd been avoiding one another. He hadn't seen her bright blond curls disappearing around the corner of her veranda or heard any screams from invading insects. Not that he wished he had…

Forcing his features into the sternest frown he could manage, he lifted his head.

"This extension cord is a fire hazard," he said, clicking his pen for emphasis and slipping it into his pocket.

Tavie huffed out a breath. "You've got some nerve coming in here, acting all official and pushing me around."

"Pointing out a code violation is hardly pushing you around. Besides, it's my job. And this—" he tapped the fire-marshal badge pinned above the pocket of his white, pleated uniform shirt "—makes *me* official."

"*Harrumph.* You were such a sweet boy. What happened?"

"I grew up." On days like this, he missed the air force. During rescue operations, rank was meaningless; pararescue jumpers like him called all the shots. Period. Even commissioned officers didn't question a PJ's authority. "Can we skip the trip down memory lane and deal with today?"

Tavie patted her helmet of dyed hair and sniffed. "But today is when you're in here wanting to deprive me—an honest, hardworking shopkeeper—of my livelihood."

He rolled his eyes heavenward and prayed for patience. Since working in the fire department satisfied his need for order and discipline, he reminded himself that he had no regrets leaving the air force with an honorable discharge. He'd dedicated nearly a decade to the military, attaining the rank of sergeant. He glanced once again at Tavie's pursed lips and narrowed eyes. Well, *almost* no regrets.

"The rules are in place to keep you and your customers safe. My job is to enforce them," he told her. Maybe that would satisfy her.

"Those extensions are only temporary until I can get Earl back here to fix everything properly. He promised to come first thing this morning, but Josiah Jones bought himself a new bass boat last night. I'll bet Earl is with that brother-in-law of his on some lake right now."

Tavie might spend her days perched on a stool in front of a cash register, but nothing got past her. If she didn't know about something, that was because it wasn't worth knowing or hadn't happened yet. Cal felt a little sorry for the feckless Earl when Tavie tracked him down. And she would. "I'm sorry about your troubles, but I can't ignore a blatant fire hazard."

"And I can't afford to let all those ice-cream treats melt, waiting for Earl to catch his quota. Which is what will happen if I unplug." She pointed to the glass-topped chest-type freezer that slid open for self-service ice-cream bars, Italian ice cups and fudge bars.

After setting the clipboard on the counter with a clatter, he pulled his wallet out of his back pocket. "How much are the items in there worth?"

Tavie eyed him suspiciously. "Why? You plan on buying them? All of them?"

Cal shrugged. When you came across an immovable object like Tavie Whatley, the best way to handle it was to go around said object. So what if residents chuckled and labeled him a pushover when this got out? And this incident would crisscross the tight-knit community faster than Loon Lake's own Martin Evers's racing pigeons. "You're my last stop for today, so I'll take them over to Camp Life Launch. I'm sure the kids will make quick work of them."

Cal admired his friends for the work they were doing, giving opportunities to children who might not otherwise have them. The popularity and reputation of their operation had grown, and thanks to the grant money Mary was always chasing down, most sessions were at capacity.

Instead of using her past as an excuse not to be fully engaged in the present or future, Mary had used her experiences to leave her mark on today and help a future generation. What was he doing besides using his past as an excuse for avoiding committing to a relationship?

"Now that's the sweet boy I remember." Tavie reached over and squeezed his cheek between her thumb and forefinger. "Speaking of which, I heard you volunteered to cochair the committee for this year's town fundraiser. Good for you."

Each year the town sponsored a fundraiser to support a worthy local cause. This year they'd voted to donate the money raised so Camp Life Launch could expand. The Wilsons were hoping to add another bunkhouse to increase the number of campers. Ex-army friends of Brody were volunteering their time as counselors and mentors for the older kids during the camping sessions and even traveling to promote the organization and accompanying groups of children to Vermont.

It was definitely a worthy cause, but... *Volunteered?* He huffed out a breath. More like strong-armed by his so-called friend Liam. He rubbed the spot Tavie had pinched. How bad could being cochair be? Ellie was the other cochair, had been for years, which meant she knew what to do and when to do it. As Liam had pointed out, Cal was accustomed to following orders, doing heavy lifting and faking a smile while doing them. Of course, that last bit had earned Liam an elbow jab. Instead of setting Tavie straight about his supposed magnanimous gesture, Cal mumbled something about being happy to do his part. He just hoped he wouldn't run into Olive, Ellie's new friend, too much—not that he would, if the last week was anything to go by.

"Tell you what. I'll split the cost of the ice cream with you." Tavie climbed off her stool. "Wholesale."

"Thanks." As his nana would say, barking dogs seldom bit. Of course, that adage now applied to him, but he could live with that. He'd had a soft spot for Tavie ever since his life had imploded at age fifteen. Tavie could have turned her back, but she hadn't and had made sure no one else did, either.

And when she saw he was going down a wrong path by skipping school and letting his grades slip, she and her husband, Ogle, had put him to work in the store and the garage, giving him some purpose.

He pushed aside unwelcome memories and cleared his throat. "Do you have an empty carton or something I can put everything in?"

She stepped around the counter. "I'll do you one better and let you take some Styrofoam coolers I have in the back. Just be sure to return 'em when you're done. Deal?"

"Deal," he said and followed her into a storeroom.

After spreading goodwill in the form of ice cream to the campers and playing soccer with the Wilsons' three-year-old son, Elliott, Cal headed home. He made the turn onto his street with the enticing smell of pepperoni wafting from the take-out pizza on his passenger seat and Ellie Goulding's breathy voice coming from his speakers.

As if he'd conjured her up with his contemplation of the home, the Victorian's current owner stepped onto that veranda and Cal's foot hit the brake. He cursed as his pickup rocked to a stop in the middle of the street and the pizza box slid onto the floor.

"Damn," he muttered under his breath and eased his foot off the brake.

The sight of her snatched his breath away. Like a blow to the chest. Every. Damn. Time. She'd been on his mind since that very first night at Hennen's. The cookout hadn't helped, either, since he'd watched her playing with his friends' kids. How natural she'd looked with them.

Olive wasn't tall, about half a foot shorter than his six foot two, but those impossibly long legs grabbed his attention. Almost as much as that tumbled mass of golden curls. Although he couldn't see them from this distance, he knew her eyes weren't simply brown, but honey gold. She wasn't a classical beauty, but Olive was striking nonetheless.

Which aggravated and annoyed him beyond reason. And messed with his equilibrium.

He'd run into a teller from the bank on the green two days ago while shopping at the Pic-N-Save and she'd asked when they were getting together again. He'd taken her out once, had an okay time and had thought about temporarily exploring any chemistry… until that night, when he'd met Olive.

He pulled his truck into his driveway and shook his head. Why her? She was the last woman he wanted to be attracted to. They shared the same circle of friends, and according to them, the woman believed in fairy-tale endings. Probably why she thought she could take on that house all by herself. Now she was on the hunt for someone to help with repairs, to fall in love with, a man of her dreams to help her fill those bedrooms with children. *Right?*

His conscience pricked him because Olive wasn't predatory, but a guy needed some sort of defense against her, so he'd labeled her a man hunter, deservedly or not. If she'd been looking for a good time, no strings attached, he was her man. Unfortunately, she had soccer games and minivans written all over her.

He cut the Tacoma's engine in the middle of Goulding's "Anything Could Happen." Reaching down, he grabbed the pizza box from the floor and caught Olive's reflection in the rearview mirror as he sat back up. She was sashaying across her front lawn toward the fire hydrant on the corner, a folded newspaper under her arm and a can of paint in her hand.

He set the box on the seat, his gaze glued to the mirror. "Oh, Olive, tell me you're not going to do what I think you are," he muttered under his breath.

Squatting down, she spread out the newspaper on the ground next to the fire hydrant and began prying the lid off the can. Cursing, Cal scrambled out of the black pickup and slammed the driver's door. First Tavie and now his alluring—but off-limits— neighbor. Couldn't a guy catch a break?

She glanced in his direction and her smile faded as he sprinted across the street that separated their houses. That was a good thing, he told himself, because her full-wattage smile needed a warning label. A guy didn't stand a chance against that glow.

He might know on an intellectual level they didn't fit as a couple, but he still had to fight the physical pull. After all, he was a thirty-five-year-old man with a healthy libido and Olive was…well, Olive. Maybe he should help her find someone. He didn't poach, so that would put her out of reach.

She set the lid from the paint can on the newspaper as he slammed to a halt in front of her.

He looked down and grimaced. Just as he suspected. The can contained bright red paint. Some might even call it fire-engine red.

"Olive…" he began, but had to clear the raspiness from his voice before he could continue. "You can't do that."

She rose with a graceful unfolding of those legs and faced him. "Come to scold me about breaking more of your precious codes?"

"As a matter of fact, I am. And they're not *mine*—" he rested his hands on his hips "—but it *is* my job to enforce them."

She narrowed her eyes and lifted her chin. "And what is it you think I'm going to do?"

God, but she looked even more beautiful when annoyed. Those eyes sparkled and color rose in those cheeks. Normally, he'd be looking for an escape from an angry woman, but with her he had to fight the urge to lean closer, to get under her skin even further to see her reaction.

Calling himself all kinds of names, he pointed one of his black Corcoran leather boots toward the opened can. "Looks to me like you're planning to paint the fire hydrant."

"And what if I am? It's in my yard, and it's well past time someone did. Frankly, it's a rusty eyesore."

Ignoring the quick and pleasant jolt from the sparks emanating from those golden eyes, he nodded. "All of that may be true, but homeowners can't paint them."

"Why not?" She scowled, causing a little dimple to form in the middle of her forehead.

His fingers itched to explore that dimple or maybe put his tongue— *Jeez. Knock it off. Focus.* What were they talking...ah, yes, the fire hydrant. He sighed. It really was unsightly. "Because it's the utility company's responsibility to paint them in coordination with the fire department."

Her face cleared and brightened. "Then I'm just saving them a step."

He shook his head. "The body, bonnet and cap are color-coded to relay information to firefighters about the size of the water main, the pressure and whether or not they might have to flush debris from the hydrant before hooking up their hoses."

She gave him a side-eye glance. "Are you making all that up?"

"Sorry, Olive. As much as I enjoy ruining your plans, at the moment I'm just doing my job."

"You don't have to look so smug while doing it." She thrust out her lower lip.

"Can't help it." He hooked his thumbs into his front pockets to keep his hands occupied, working to tame the urge to stroke her mouth and maybe do more. Safer that way. "After a day spent hassling old ladies and terrifying young children, disappointing you is just icing on the cake," he said drily.

Of course, he'd be the one getting hassled and terrified if Tavie caught him referring to her as an old lady. He could picture the shopkeeper boxing his ears and, for the second time that day, a spontaneous grin spread across his face. This time he didn't have a clipboard to hide behind. Nor did he feel inclined to hide it. Which meant he was treading in dangerous territory with his lovely neighbor.

And he wasn't sure how he felt about that.

Despite having her plans disrupted, Olive felt her lips crook upward until she was flashing her own grin in response to Cal's crooked one. She'd heard that her way-too-sexy neighbor had spent part of his afternoon with the kids at Camp Life Launch. She'd stopped at the general store on the way home from work and Tavie had recounted the entire incident. And his once pristine white uniform shirt—yeah, she'd stood in the window and watched him leave for work that morning—bore the evidence of his activities. Not only was it wrinkled, but it also sported a grass stain and a smear of chocolate ice cream.

Why did he have to do that to her? Make her react in ways she didn't want to? It was hard not to be attracted when he looked as though he'd enjoyed himself as much as the kids. And she needed to harden her heart because, according to their mutual friends, Cal Pope was not a forever guy, a man who wanted children of his own. Call her naive, but forever was what she longed for. Home, marriage, family. Those three formed a unit that she considered unique and precious, and she'd been in mourning since the day it had all been snatched from her at the loss of her parents when she was eleven. The hopes she'd had for creating a family of her own one day had died with the end of her engagement to Kurt.

As for Cal, she'd heard about his dad swindling people and running off with his secretary, but she wasn't sure that explained his aversion to commitment. There might be more to the story, but she didn't want to pump Tavie or any of her friends for information. She didn't want to advertise her interest in Cal.

"Earth to Olive." *Snap. Snap.* "Are we in agreement?"

Caught daydreaming about a nonexistent future, she felt herself blush. She needed to stop thinking about him in those terms, because as she'd been planning, he'd been snapping his fingers. Which perfectly summed up their relationship. Relationship? *As if.* They were acquaintances, no more. She could only hope her face wasn't as red as it felt as she pulled herself back to the present. "Agreement about what?"

He hitched his chin toward her painting supplies. "You'll leave the fire hydrant alone?"

She sighed. Yeah, totally different wavelengths. "You really know how to spoil a girl's fun."

"Spoiling fun? Yeah, it's why I get out of bed every morning."

She glanced across the street at his colonial blue clapboard house. The place where he slept every night. Was he the type to wear pajamas, or did he—

What is wrong with you? Get those dangerous thoughts out of your head right now.

"Well, I'm glad I give you a reason to get up," she said, unable to keep the sarcasm out of her tone. Maybe if he wasn't so damn sexy, she wouldn't include him in her daydreams.

She hunkered down to put the lid back on the paint can. She'd find some other use for the paint. Lord knew, the house needed enough repairs and renovations to keep her busy for a lifetime. This experience with the fire hydrant told her she needed to put more effort into research before tackling her renovations. She knew Cal had recently spruced up his place, so he might be a good source of information. But did she want to ask him? Brody might be more help. He'd done a lot of restoration work on his farmhouse, both before and after he and Mary had gotten together. Between the two of them, she could get tips on renovation *and* running a business.

Cal shifted his feet and she glanced up. Was he blushing? What had she said to make him react like that? The last thing she'd said was… *Oh.* "Huh… now that I think about what I said, it may have sounded—"

"I know what you meant, Olive." He ran a hand through his dark, unruly hair. "I didn't take it any other way."

Oh, what she wouldn't give to trail her fingers through those thick ebony waves, muss him up even more. She was the newcomer to town and to the group, so their loyalty would naturally be with Cal. Painful experience had taught her what happened to mutual friends when couples went their separate ways. And she'd be the loser. Again.

To be fair, Ellie and Mary were too nice to ghost her, but their husbands might be a different story. She and the women might continue to do things together, but she doubted she'd be included in group activities like she was now. Ellie and Mary had said they were looking forward to including her in summer cookouts and skating parties by the lake in the winter. The thought of not getting to participate with her newfound companions tightened her chest.

It may have only been a short time, but she'd come to think of her small group of friends in Loon Lake as extended family.

Needing to escape her unproductive line of thinking, she sprang up. One foot went out from under her when the newspaper slid on the grass.

She started to tumble, but Cal grabbed her elbows and she landed against his chest instead of on her butt.

Oh, my. Firefighting was a physically demanding job and evidently Cal had kept up his exercise routine despite his new position as fire marshal. What she wouldn't give to have the right to melt against all that maleness and muscle.

He smelled like grass and sunshine with a touch

of chocolate. Had he enjoyed some of the ice-cream goodies? If she raised her face and kissed him, would he taste like that, too?

Disappointed because she didn't have the nerve to steal a kiss, she sighed.

"Olive? You okay?" he asked, his breath warm on her face.

If I could just stay like this for a minute or two and— She pulled away. "Of course. Thanks. Clumsy me."

He released her and took a hasty step back. Obviously, she didn't evoke any of the same physical responses in *him* as he did in her. Why him? Loon Lake might be small, but it held its share of single men. Surely some were interested in the same things she was. And if that confirmed the things Cal had said about her at the cookout, then too bad. Wanting to get married and start a family wasn't some bizarre notion, nor should her desire make her mercenary.

"Have you made any progress?"

"Progress?" *Please tell me I didn't express any of those desires aloud.*

"With your plans to reopen the B and B?"

"Oh, that. No. Your threat of a list of code violations was a bit daunting, so I've had to put those plans on the back burner at the moment," she said, unable to keep the disappointment from her voice. She wasn't sure if the emotion stemmed from having to slow down her plans to reopen the B and B or from her inconvenient attraction to Cal. "But you haven't deterred me, just made me rethink my timeline."

"I'm truly sorry." He lifted a hand as if to reach out, but let it drop without making contact. "But you wouldn't want to put yourself or any potential guests in harm's way."

Why did he have to sound so sympathetic? So nice? It was totally messing with her plan to be polite but cool. And to get past the fact he'd hurt her feelings the first time they'd been introduced. Maybe if he hadn't laughed when she had poured her heart out about her plans for her new home.

She had to give him credit for at least trying to cover his laughter. He'd made her feel naive, but she was adult enough to get over it. Wasn't she?

"No, I just need to live in it and love it as much as she did. Being able to run it as a business would be a bonus." Her gaze raked over the house. Right now, there was peeling paint, sagging porch steps and a rusty light fixture on the porch, but she imagined the porch ceiling painted light blue, the wooden posts, rails, balusters and moldings painted a creamy white, and the gingerbread trim restored and painted a complementary color. Bright white wicker furniture with blue and red throw pillows and cushions. Carriage lights hung on either side of the door, their black metal scrollwork gleaming from the lights.

"Then you're two for two."

Thinking she heard a strange gentleness in his

voice, she turned her attention back to him, but his expression gave nothing away. *Rein in your imagination*, she cautioned herself. Building castles in the air was dangerous. She'd done that with the Victorian, and though she dearly loved it, she had to admit she had no idea what the long list of repairs would ultimately look like. She needed to pull her head out of the clouds and concentrate on the known, get a list of code violations from Cal. "The home is more than I ever dreamed possible."

He glanced toward the house, his mouth tightening as his gaze wandered over it.

His reaction sent her pulse thrumming. "Yeah, I know it's more eyesore than beauty at the moment. I'm surprised the neighbors haven't gotten up a petition or something."

He turned back to her. "By neighbors, I suppose you mean me."

Warmth rose in her face. No sense denying the obvious. She looked across the street. "Your lawn doesn't even have weeds. Did you chase them all over here?"

"And if I did?"

His deep chuckle reverberated in her belly and raised the hairs on her arms. Every time she shoved her attraction to him in the box marked "off-limits" and tried to slam the lid, he pried it back open. She managed a careless shrug. "I'd be okay with it. To me, weeds are just flowers whose virtues have yet to be discovered."

"You probably even refer to weeds as wildflowers," he said in a tone used on someone who believed in fairy tales.

His comments threw her back to an incident—sadly, one of many—during her engagement to Kurt. Unlike other members of his family, her future sister-in-law had loved nothing better than to point out that Olive didn't fit in—no matter how much she tried—with the country-club set that Kurt's family called friends. Looking back, she regretted letting them make her feel less for things she'd had no control over. The way they made her feel unworthy was her fault and it was on her that she'd even made the effort. She should never have given them that power over her. As a child she'd had no choice, but as an adult she did.

She had to relax her jaw so she could speak. "You might like to denigrate wildflowers, but they grow without intervention. Whereas cultivated flowers generally need extra help to thrive."

Was that really her sounding so prim and proper?

"Is this what's referred to as getting schooled?"

What was it about this guy that brought out all sorts of conflicting feelings in her? "I'm sorry—I didn't mean to lecture. Wildflowers might not be as cultured and pretty as those cultivated ones, but that doesn't mean no one can appreciate them."

He frowned. "I won't ever look at a weed the same way again."

"Now who's getting schooled?"

"Olive…"

"All I'm asking is, don't you think it's better to go through life with a positive attitude?"

"And you obviously don't think I have a positive attitude." He quirked an eyebrow.

She hated how a simple facial expression from him could put her on the defensive. "I didn't say that."

"You just thought it." He held up his hand when she started to protest. "Don't. It's my turn to apologize for messing with you."

"So Tavie wasn't the only person you've hassled today." She was enjoying the fact she'd turned the tables on him.

"So you know about that?" He blushed and glanced away.

Despite their history, she regretted putting him on the spot and laid her hand on his arm in a friendly gesture. "I think what you did was sweet, buying half of those ice creams to help her out."

He grunted.

Huh, maybe *sweet* wasn't what a guy like Cal wanted to be called, even if it was the truth. Oh, well, a change of subject might help. "I look forward to working with you on the fundraising committee."

He turned his gaze back to her, a frown marring his forehead. "You mean Ellie. Technically, she's the one in charge. I'm more of a figurehead. I'm letting her call the shots."

She'd been honored when Ellie had asked her to take over, and she wanted to be successful, to be considered part of the Loon Lake community. She wasn't deaf to the whispers of a few who questioned whether or not she even deserved to be living in a home that she hadn't even paid for. They were definitely in the minority, though, because the majority had welcomed her to town and into their lives. But, at times, she still felt like an outsider...or a flatlander, as the locals liked to call people not native to Vermont.

And she wasn't going to let Cal's attitude ruin her chance to prove to everyone that she belonged, even if she was a newcomer.

Matching him frown for frown, she let her hand fall away from his arm. "Good for you, except there's a new sheriff in town. Or should I say committee chair, because I'm taking over for Ellie. And I'll be expecting my cochair to pull his weight."

Chapter Four

Cal shook his head. Of course, his trip to the camp with Tavie's ice cream was bound to get out. You couldn't do anything in Loon Lake without everyone knowing about it—especially if what you'd done in any way involved Tavie.

He wouldn't have cared, but what guy wanted to be labeled sweet? His actions weren't sweet. No way. He'd simply done the most expedient thing, considering the situation with Tavie and— Wait. *What?* He did a mental double take as he reviewed what Olive had just told him.

Olive was the new cochair of *his* committee? The committee he'd agreed to be on because Ellie was the other chair? Had he heard that right?

He shook his head as if that would speed up the blood flow to his sluggish brain. "But—but... Ellie. She's—"

"Not anymore. She decided to step aside and asked me to take over. I'm the new cochair." She held up her hands in a *ta-da* motion.

The bottom dropped out of his stomach as her words finally penetrated his addled brain. His slow reflexes and lowered IQ weren't his fault. How was he expected to think clearly when she'd been touching him? The effect was such that even after she'd released his arm, it had taken a moment for the blood to reenter his brain and her words to penetrate the haze. Had she reached out to him to purposely slow his reaction time? Used his body's response to her as a weapon? Had his dad's secretary used her age and looks to lure in his father? He'd heard that more than once from his mother after his dad's disappearance. He wasn't sure he was convinced of the validity of it. His father acted of his own free will. The man he'd grown up with had been strong-willed enough not to have been led around by anyone, male or female.

"I assured her I'd be happy to take over and assume her responsibilities," she said, filling the silence.

Oh, man, now she was using that whole face smile thing. Did she know how that turned his brain to mush? On a scale of bad things, the idea of spending hours planning a local event with his beautiful and cheerful new neighbor was, like, the worst. Next, she'd have him wondering if maybe his married friends were the lucky ones, as if maybe they knew something he didn't. No. Thinking like that was dangerous. His mom had tied her happiness to his dad and look how that turned out. His mother had thought marriage was the ticket to contentment. His mom claimed her husband's actions had stolen her ability to feel joy or hold her head high when people questioned how much she'd profited herself from her husband's embezzlement. The authorities couldn't find anything to connect her to his crimes, but the shadow of suspicion followed her. He needed to be stronger than Olive's touches, her smiles, made him feel.

"I see," he said. Well, wasn't he just the master of the snappy comeback? Surely, he could come up with something better. Evidently not, because he searched his blood-deprived brain again and came up with absolutely nothing.

This shouldn't be happening. He was supposed to be spending less time with Olive, not more. The more time he spent with her showed him the attraction went beyond anything physical, which he'd shared with numerous women in the past, like that bank teller. Olive was funny, thoughtful, a genuinely nice person, and hurting her was the last thing he wanted. And he would hurt her if things got out of hand because they wanted different things.

He could always step down from the committee. Liam would hassle him, for sure, but he could handle that. But did he actually *want* to step down? Sure, he'd given his pal a hard time when he'd asked him to represent the fire department on the committee, but he'd seen this opportunity as a chance to give back to the town. And he believed in what the Wilsons were doing with Camp Life Launch, the children they were helping. If he could help raise more money so they could help more children, then he'd do his best.

Everyone could have turned their backs on him and his mother after Dear Old Dad had done a runner with his secretary and his investment clients' money, but they hadn't. Thanks in part to Tavie Whatley and her exerting her influence over others. Sure, some people had looked at him and his mom with disdain or pity, and he couldn't blame them for either. People who'd invested with his father had lost lots of money, some even their life savings. Looking back, he should be grateful he and his mother hadn't been run out of town on a rail. Maybe the fact that his father had run off with Charlotte Johnson had helped. He was sure women could sympathize with his mother's humiliation at having her husband abandon her for someone half his age.

What if he got taken in again? Could Cal really trust his judgment enough to commit to anyone long-term? Trust a relationship enough to bring a child of his own into the world?

"…does that sound?"

Olive's question brought him out of his reverie. *Not good, Pope, not good.* He needed to pay attention, be in control of *all* of his faculties whenever she spoke. No telling what she'd have him doing otherwise. "I'm sorry. What?"

"I said I've been jotting down ideas in a special notebook." She lifted a shoulder and used it to swipe at a curl stuck to her cheek with sweat. "It's practically full already. Since I won't be painting this hydrant after all, would you like to come in and discuss them?"

A *special* notebook? What did that even mean? And what sort of ideas did she have? He glanced across the street. To his truck. To his pizza, sitting in his car. To his safe, simple, solitary life. "Well, I…"

"We could go over my notes, get your input. I'm sure you have a lot of ideas, too."

"Not a one," he muttered without thinking. Now those honey-gold eyes were narrowed, making him regret his honesty. Looked like today was his day for annoying the women in his life.

"Oh, I find that hard to believe," she said, and her face smoothed out. "I'd love to hear any thoughts you have. I don't want you to think I'm trying to take over."

Take over. Be my guest, he thought, but knew better than to voice that. After all, he did have some self-preservation instincts…as long as she wasn't touching him and scrambling his brain.

"Ellie said Liam was going to mention it to you, so I assumed you already knew."

"I only spoke to Liam briefly this morning. He got called to Burlington to work on a suspected arson case." *Pretty convenient, McBride.*

"Oh. Then I'm sorry to spring it on you like this." Her tone may have conveyed contrition, but her expression indicated the opposite.

He caught the twitch of her lips, as if she was repressing a smile, and pounced. "Are you? Or are you enjoying telling me and paying me back for not letting you paint the hydrant?"

The smile broke through. "Caught me."

"I thought you looked a bit smug," he said, relieved to have the mood lightened. Arguing with Olive was the last thing he wanted. Fights could create sparks and one little spark was all that was needed to create an inferno between them and make him kiss her senseless.

"Pot? Kettle?" she asked.

"Contrary to popular belief, I don't enjoy giving you—or anyone—bad news." And that was definitely the truth. He might get some pleasure out of teasing her, but he didn't enjoy spoiling her plans.

She tilted her head. "I believe you. Truce?"

"I didn't realize we were feuding but okay. Truce." He took the hand she offered, telling himself he could handle this—this…attraction or whatever it was. He gave her hand a brief shake and tucked his now tingling one in his pocket, out of trouble.

"So would you like to come in? We can sit in the parlor and—"

"Let me get this straight," he interrupted, quirking an eyebrow. "You're inviting me into your parlor?"

"Yes, but I— Oh! I get it. The spider and the fly. You're familiar with it?" She giggled. "Don't tell me you've been attending story hour at the library?"

At his age, giggling women weren't his thing, but with Olive he found he wanted to join in and laugh and enjoy the moment. "I haven't, but evidently Elliott Wilson has because he was telling me all about the spider and the fly today. Brody kindly translated when I thought he was talking about a new Power Ranger instead of an old-time term for a living room."

"I'm glad to know I'm not the only one who sometimes needs Brody or Mary to translate Elliott-speak. But he's such a little cutie, I love talking to him." She scratched her nose, leaving behind a streak of fire-engine-red paint from the brush still in her hand. "I'm still getting used to having a parlor as opposed to a simple living room. Some of the ladies at Sunshine Gardens set me straight."

"What about a veranda?" he asked, nodding toward the porch. He twitched, barely restraining his desire to wipe off the smudge with his thumb.

She followed his gaze with hers. "You mean my porch?"

"That's too impressive to be called a porch… I like the word *veranda*." Oh, man, what was he doing rattling on about veranda versus porch and sounding like his nana? But Olive could make almost anything, even mundane architecture discussions, interesting, he realized.

"I do, too." She nodded her head once. "So did you want to come in or do you have plans?"

He'd planned on catching the second game of today's doubleheader. But he found himself wanting to linger, stay with her, even if it was just standing here, talking about nothing in particular.

The silence stretched, though, and he was both happy and disappointed when she stooped to gather her painting supplies. "Don't worry about it. This will give me time to type up my notes. That way you won't have to try to decipher my chicken scratching. I'll let you know once I get my notes together."

"I, uh… I stopped and picked up a pizza on the way home. We could share it. If you really wanted to show me those notes…now." Could he sound any less inviting? He desperately wanted to share a slice with her, though, even if all they were doing was talking about the fundraiser.

She smiled but this one was just a slight curve of her lips and didn't involve any of the rest of her. "No thanks. I already ate, but maybe some other time."

"Yeah. Sure." He didn't have to sound so relieved, even though he was actually a bit bummed that she turned him down. What was it about her that made him act like this? He was usually pretty straightforward in his dealings with the opposite sex.

She started back toward the house. As he slipped his hand into his pocket, he found a wadded-up napkin he'd shoved in there while handing out ice cream at Brody's. "Olive, wait."

She stopped and swung back around. "Yes?"

He held out the napkin. "You've got paint—" he pressed an index finger to the end of his nose "—right there."

"Thanks." She shrugged and shifted the paint can.

"Wait. Let me," he said and approached her.

Cal took the napkin in one hand and cupped her chin with the other. Her skin was soft, and when he angled her head, he got a whiff of something. Lavender? For a moment he stood frozen, her chin in his grasp, her breath on his hand. He stared into her eyes and noticed a darker gold ring around the irises.

His gaze drifted to her mouth. Her very desirable, kissable mouth. All he had to do was lean forward to put his lips to hers—

She blinked and broke the spell. He cleared his throat and began swabbing the paint spot. "You'll probably need to use soap and water to get the rest, but I got some of it."

He dropped his hand and took a half step back, as if in self-defense.

"I'd better do that now or I might have to scrape it off."

He was tempted to tell her not to bother. She looked kind of cute with that dab of paint, but not saying that was a much wiser choice. Even wiser was not following the impulse to taste her lips. And from now on, he was making *only* wise choices around Olive Downing.

Olive scrubbed the paint off her face after returning inside. Once again, she'd managed to make a fool of herself in front of Cal. He'd offered to share his pizza, and she'd somehow managed to resist the chance to be closer to him.

"How was I supposed to know you couldn't paint a fire hydrant, even if it was on your property?" she asked her reflection. *I could have done some basic research*, she admitted ruefully to herself. *That might be necessary. Especially since Cal seems to know his way around the rules...*

He certainly liked his regulations. She shouldn't find that sexy, but somehow did.

She laughed. She never would have considered herself a rule breaker. Quite the opposite, as a matter of fact. In school she'd always kept her head down, fearing someone might notice her and point her out as a foster kid. She remembered one girl had gotten slapped with that label and others looked askance at her. As if she'd done something to deserve what had happened to her, with her losing her biological family. She'd felt excluded and had cherished the few friends she did have even more ever since.

As an adult, she could look back and understand part of the hazing could have stemmed from fear. She was a reminder that it could happen to them.

After getting the paint off her face, she went into the kitchen. She'd lied to Cal about having already eaten supper. She wasn't proud of that fact, but she'd known he'd only issued the invitation out of politeness. She could tell he hadn't really wanted her to accept, and she was determined not to throw herself at him. Pride could be so inconvenient. Without it, she might be sharing a pizza—or maybe something more—with him right now.

Instead, she opened the refrigerator and took out leftover chicken and dumplings she'd made in the slow cooker the previous day. By the end of the week, she knew she'd be sick of the leftovers, but she'd been taught not to waste food. With one of her foster families, you ate what was on your plate or you didn't eat at the next meal.

While her supper was heating up, she put water in the electric kettle for a cup of tea. The electricity then suddenly went off as she was getting out a mug and tea bag.

"Great. What's wrong now?"

She glanced at the clock on the stove, but it was still working. So not all electricity was out, just the microwave and kettle. She must have tripped a circuit breaker.

She grabbed the flashlight she kept on the counter and opened the door to the basement. Wrinkling her nose at the musty odor, she started down the wooden steps. She was grateful once again that the previous owner had installed the washer and dryer in the utility room off the back of the house. The basement was not her favorite part of the home.

"I'm an adult. I can handle this," she said and made her way down the stairs.

Cal got the pizza out of the truck, slamming the passenger door harder than necessary in the process. But it felt good to take his frustration out on something. Inside, he set the box on the counter in the kitchen. After getting a dish out of the cupboard, he tossed a slice of the now cold food on it and put it in the microwave. Not the best choice for reheating, but at the moment he didn't care. While his dinner was getting zapped, he pulled a beer from the refrigerator and popped off the cap.

He sank down on the couch, unlaced his boots and pulled them off. Each one made a *thunk* as they landed on the floor beside the sofa. He wiggled his toes and put his socked feet up on the coffee table next to the plate he'd grabbed from the microwave. His most recent interaction with Olive flashed through his mind; he remembered her charming smile with a surge of desire.

He pulled his phone from his pocket and called Liam. He sipped on the beer while he waited for the call to connect.

"Hey, Cal, I was going to call this evening," Liam said by way of greeting.

"Is that when you were going to tell me?"

Liam's sigh came through the phone. "Ah. I see you found out. How did—"

"I got it straight from Olive's mouth." He had to suppress the groan that tried to escape as his mind went directly to thoughts of her luscious mouth and what those lips would feel like under his.

"Then I didn't need to worry about calling you. Bridget, give your brother back his truck, please."

Despite his annoyance, or maybe because of it, Cal grinned at the chaos he imagined at Liam's house. It sounded nice…but he dismissed the thought. He took another sip of beer and swallowed. "You could have given me a heads-up."

"I meant to but— Sean, don't hit your sister."

"You got everything under control there?"

"Yeah, just the usual chaos," Liam said and sighed. "As I said, I meant to call you. I guess I should have done it from the office. Sean, that belongs to your sister. Put it back."

Cal heard squabbling in the background. "Dude, look, if this is a bad time…"

"When you're the parent of two-year-old twins, I'm not sure there's ever a good time."

"Very active twins," Cal added and chuckled. "Is that why Ellie is stepping down from the committee?"

"Not necessarily. This is more about Ellie than Sean and Bridget."

"Ellie?" Sitting up straighter, Cal grew serious. "Liam, is Ellie okay?"

Cal had been serving overseas when Liam and Ellie had gotten together, but from what he gathered, the road to their happiness had had some bumps. Liam had lost his mother and a friend to cancer, and Ellie had been in remission for years, and his friend had had to work through his fears before he and Ellie found happiness together.

"She's not sick. Not like what you're thinking, anyway," Liam said. "We—we, uh, hadn't wanted to say anything yet but she's pregnant again."

"That's terrific. Congratulations," Cal said and meant it. Not wanting any kids of his own didn't mean he didn't like them. He simply didn't want to be responsible for someone else's well-being and happiness. His father had failed him, and he refused to be the cause of someone else's pain, let alone his own offspring's.

"Thanks. We're excited but right now she's exhausted. As you pointed out, Sean and Bridget are pretty active toddlers as it is."

"Is there anything I can do to help?"

"Just play nice with Olive on this committee thing. Ellie hated giving it up. You know how much she believes in this, and she hated relinquishing her duties as chair, but I urged her to. I could see how much the pregnancy was zapping her strength right now."

Cal grimaced and gave up his plan to bow out. He didn't want to do anything to cause undue stress on Ellie. He was an adult and could handle being around Olive. Couldn't he?

"And Olive is the perfect choice to replace her. After all, she's an activities director at the senior center and good at organizing, so she'll be able to handle this, no problem. Ellie says she's confident Olive will be great and she's the only reason Ellie agreed to hand over the reins."

"Didn't you say you urged her? I would have thought that was enough to make her give it up, bowing to your infinite wisdom. Didn't you point that out?"

Liam chuckled. "I want to be around when you fall. Because you're gonna fall hard and I want to be there to witness it."

Cal held up a hand as if stopping traffic, even though he knew Liam couldn't see him. "Not me," he insisted. "Never gonna happen."

"Never say never, friend," Liam said.

"Uh-huh. That's one thing I can guarantee."

Liam laughed. "Famous last words. I believe I might've said the same at some point."

"It's true." He was pretty sure he had to believe in happily-ever-after before he aspired to it. And he most definitely didn't believe in it. His mother had eventually driven everyone away with her bitterness. Even after the statute of limitations had expired on his crimes, Dear Old Dad never bothered to get in touch with him.

"Sure, whatever you say. So we're good? You'll play nice with Olive?"

"You can count on me," Cal assured him before they said their goodbyes and he disconnected the call.

He tossed the phone onto the couch and rubbed a hand over his face. Maybe this committee thing wasn't going to be the walk in the park he'd assumed when Ellie was in charge, but it wasn't anything he couldn't handle. He could be attracted to Olive all he wanted, but he just wouldn't act on it.

That decided, he took a bite of pizza as his doorbell chimed. Great. Maybe he'd ignore it. Yeah, that thought lasted about thirty seconds. After taking another bite, he set his supper back on the plate and headed for the door.

Swallowing the food in his mouth, he opened the door, determined to get rid of whoever was standing on the other side. It was Olive.

"Hi." She wrung her hands and inhaled deeply. "I'm really sorry to bother you, but I have a problem and didn't know who else to turn to."

He swung the door open wider. "C'mon in."

"Well, I, um…" She stepped inside, glanced at his feet and blushed.

He looked down at his feet and checked for holes in his socks. No, all good there. So why was she turning such a bright shade of red? She couldn't possibly be having the same lustful thoughts he had when he looked at her. Could she?

She's looking at your feet, you dope. What kind of thoughts could they trigger? Unless… No. Women didn't actually believe that old wives' tale about the size of a guy's feet. Did they?

Didn't matter. It was best to get those sorts of thoughts out of his head. He cleared his throat. "Olive? You said you had a problem?"

"What?" Her head popped up. "Oh. Yeah, I thought I blew a circuit breaker. I had the microwave and the electric teakettle on at the same time. That used to happen at my old place, too. And that apartment was a lot newer than this one, so I guess I should have known better."

Her rambling betrayed her nervousness. Was she using this lame excuse to get him to come to her rescue? Yeah, he needed to get over himself. "You don't know how to reset a circuit breaker?"

"Oh, no, I do. It's not like it's hard. And I actually found what I think is the electrical box in the basement but something's wrong."

"What do you mean?"

"There's no—" she made a motion with her hands "—no levers to push. Just a bunch of weird-looking circle thingies."

"That's the fuse box," he explained, but her expression didn't change. "Your electrical wiring apparently hasn't been updated."

She began to gnaw on her lower lip, and he found himself wishing he'd given in to temptation and kissed her earlier. At least he'd know what that lip felt and tasted like. Huh. Maybe it was better not to know these things. He shifted his stance. "Didn't someone show this to you when you took possession of the home? Explain the old wiring?"

She shook her head. "The former owner's great-nephew, Randall Pickard, met me at his lawyer's office and just handed me the keys. I think Mr. Pickard was still angry over having to turn the home over to me. He refused to take me on a walk-through. I may not have ever owned a home before, but I know how real-estate transactions work and inquired about one."

He nodded. Olive might be optimistic and even a little naive, but she wasn't dumb. "You blew a fuse."

"Well, no. Not really. I was very polite even when the former owner's great-nephew sneered, called me a derogatory name and said he'd take repossession of the house within six months because I didn't look capable of hanging on to it."

Cal clenched his fist. If this had been anyone else, he'd probably find the humor in her misinterpretation of his observation. But he was having trouble because he hated the idea of anyone disrespecting Olive. Sure, he enjoyed teasing her, but he would never do anything malicious. Or anything to make her feel…well, less than. He knew all too well, from the side looks he'd gotten after his father had left, how that felt.

If Sadie Pickard's great-nephew had been here, he'd haul off and pop him on the jaw for treating Olive like that. Swallowing his anger because it wasn't directed at her and he didn't want her to think it was, he said, "I meant your electrical fuses."

At her blank look, he sighed. "You have fuses. That's what blew. Blowing a fuse is the equivalent of tripping a circuit breaker."

"So that's where that saying comes from. Huh. I guess that makes sense, although I doubt my appliances got angry." She blushed again. "You probably agree with Pickard about my abilities."

"Absolutely not." He reached out and touched her arm, steeling himself against the little jolt he knew he would get from touching her. The reaction was worth it if it helped her. "Only people past a certain age remember fuses. Most homes these days have been updated to have circuit breakers. No reason for you to feel embarrassed."

"Still…" She shook her head. "I should've looked it up on the internet before coming over here and bothering you."

"It's no bother. I don't mind." He gently squeezed her arm before letting go. "Honest. Let me get my shoes on and I'll help you look for a replacement fuse. Hopefully Pickard didn't toss them before handing the place over."

"I wouldn't put it past him."

"We'll take a look. I imagine Sadie would have kept spares. If not, I promise we'll track some down for you."

A look passed over her face that had him wanting to touch her again. Touch? *Ha!* In fact, he wanted to do a lot more than that. He pulled on his boots and yanked on the laces as he did them up.

Outside, he went to the driveway and opened the stainless-steel tool chest he'd installed in the bed of his truck. Retrieving the large lantern-style flash-light from it, he checked to be sure the batteries were still good.

"The lights in my basement still work. It's just parts of the kitchen that aren't," she said as they started crossing the street to her home.

"I like being prepared," he told her.

She half turned to him as they crossed the street. "I'll bet you were a Boy Scout."

He clenched his jaw. Yeah, he'd been a Scout. That activity had been one of the things he and his dad had shared. He'd have been lost when it came to things like the Pinewood Derby if not for his father. They'd worked his car until it had been a work of art. At least in the mind of a seven-year-old. Though that bond hadn't lasted.

Rubbing his chest, he wondered how long it had

been since he'd been able to come up with a pleasant memory involving his father. He'd been well on his way to making Eagle Scout, but the bitterness he'd felt at his father's betrayal had him not even wanting to be involved in something he'd spent so much time on with his dad. He'd dropped out of the Scouts entirely.

"Cal?"

He blinked as Olive's voice penetrated the red haze that had taken over in his brain. "I'm sorry. What?"

"I was asking about the fuses. Why would I have those?"

"Because your place hasn't had any updating," he said, glad to be focusing on the present.

"But what about all your fire codes? Didn't the previous owner have to follow them?"

He couldn't help but smile at her insistence that the fire codes belonged to him. Instead of finding that annoying, he found it...endearing. He swallowed the groan that bubbled up. When had he turned into the kind of guy who used words like *endearing*?

"Cal?"

"Sorry." *Get your head out of the clouds.* He needed to focus on the here and now before he embarrassed himself by saying something stupid in front of Olive. "Sadie had obviously closed the B and B before she had to make those sorts of changes."

"Maybe that's why she closed it. She was forced

to. Hmm?" She gave him a mock scowl, but the effect was ruined because her lips kept curving up at the corners.

"Don't look at me. That was way before my time as fire marshal." He held up his hands palms out as they walked along the brick sidewalk to the Victorian. All the weeds that had been choking the walkway were gone and the bricks looked scrubbed. Had she done that? "Nice job with the bricks, by the way."

"Changing the subject?" She tilted her head to the side as she studied him.

Her fresh scent filled his senses and he had to work hard to concentrate on their conversation. "I would if I thought it would help, but I think you're determined to blame me for these fire codes."

He'd tried to sound offended but was pretty sure he hadn't pulled it off because her lips had stopped twitching and were now turned upward in a grin. A grin that sent a shot of adrenaline—and something more—straight to his heart.

Chapter Five

Olive opened the front door, stepped inside and waited for Cal. She was still berating herself for her reaction to seeing him without his shoes on. Talk about a silly schoolgirl reaction. But the fact he'd been in his stocking feet had made the encounter feel intimate. She couldn't explain her reaction other than to call it childish.

She shut the door and realized he was standing in the deep, narrow foyer, looking around as if his head was on a swivel.

"Wow. This is wonderful. The woodwork is amazing." He wandered over to the bottom of the stairs and rubbed his palm over the dark surface of the ornately carved large starting newel. "And you're lucky it hasn't been painted over."

The staircase made two turns, one at the bottom with a square landing, and halfway up it turned with another landing and a stained glass window.

"Have you never been in here before?" she asked, surprised, though not sure why. Cal probably hadn't known Sadie all that well.

He shook his head. "The B and B has been closed for several decades and I had no cause to come here while it was Sadie's home."

"I'd love to show you around. At the moment, it's sparsely furnished. I think her great-nephew must have sold some of the furniture." Despite its current state of disrepair, she was proud of her home.

"Was he allowed to do that?"

"Sell the furniture?" She shrugged. "The attorney insisted they followed the will."

Cal muttered something under his breath about Sadie's ungrateful great-nephew. "Well, let's get the fuse changed and then you can show me around."

"Sounds like a plan. The entrance to the basement is at the back of the house by the kitchen."

He fell into step beside her as she followed the high-ceilinged hallway toward the kitchen. Just before they reached it, she stopped and opened the interior door to the basement. A musty odor hit her as she hesitated in the doorway.

"I don't come down here much," she said and tried to suppress her automatic shiver as she glanced down the staircase. The fixture near the bottom only threw off minimal light. She made a mental note to re-place the dim bulb with something brighter, possi-bly a spotlight.

He reached up and placed his index finger on the end of her nose. "Olive Downing, are you telling me you're afraid of this basement?"

"Absolutely not!" *Paper over the truth much, Olive?* "I—I just don't have a reason to come down here much."

He gently rubbed the finger across her nose. "Uh-huh."

"It's the truth," she protested.

He started to grin, and she swatted away his fin-ger but immediately regretted it. She liked having him touch her, even if it was in just a playful way, and did mess with her IQ and left her feeling breath-less. "Did you know that sixty-two percent of pro-spective home buyers say they would buy a haunted house?"

"That's interesting but I think you're stalling. Do you want me to go down by myself?"

"I'll go with you." She stuck out her chin. "It's my home."

"Your secret is safe with me." He reached out and brushed a stray curl off her cheek, tucking it behind her ear. As he leaned in, she felt the overwhelming of wanting to be kissed by him. He tipped up her chin, his dark eyes wide and staring straight at her, and then pulled back. Disappointed, she reminded herself she'd decided not to get involved with this man for a reason, and he most definitely was *not* going to start things going in the wrong direction with a passionate kiss. No matter how much she wanted to.

With a visible effort, he straightened up and pulled back. "C'mon, let's go and get this over with," she said hurriedly, turning to head down the stairs. The sooner they could forget that awkward moment, the better.

"Wait…" He put a hand on her arm. "I'll lead the way in case there's any spiders."

"Very funny." But she let him lead the way nonetheless, somehow both amused and touched by his gesture. Besides, he had the flashlight.

The wooden steps creaked as they descended to a cement floor that had mildew cracks snaking off into various directions.

"Some of these steps have a bit of give to them," he said as he reached the bottom.

"I noticed that and have already added that to my list."

"Be careful until they're repaired." He stepped on the cement floor and glanced back at her. "I'll measure them later. I have wood left over from projects at my place."

"Thank you."

"So, is there someplace or something that might hold extra fuses?"

"There's a workbench over there. I think it had

some of those plastic-bin storage drawers under it."
She had come down here twice in the weeks since
she'd moved in but hadn't lingered. She'd come the
first time to prove—to herself—that she could. The
boys at one of the homes had thought it fun to shut
her in a closet under the stairs in the basement every
chance they got and threatened her if she told. The
foster mother had scolded Olive afterward, saying
she was too old for such nonsense when she began
to balk at going into the cellar. Although that foster
situation and those cruel children were well back in
her past, evidently she hadn't overcome all her fears.

He followed her over to a long wooden table with
hand tools and glass baby-food jars full of nails and
screws.

She opened the drawer and pulled out a road
map. Yellowed and torn, it must have dated from
the 1950s.

"So the fuses are old?" she asked.

"Yes." He opened drawers on the other side of
the workbench.

"I guess since you know all about them, it makes
you old." She couldn't ignore the urge to tease him.

He narrowed his eyes at her. "It's my job."

"I see." She licked her lips. Maybe teasing him
hadn't been such a smart move.

"I could shut you down right now."

She glanced at him to see if he was joking, and a
glint in his eye and a quirk to his lips indicated he

was. Who would have thought that Cal Pope, gruff neighbor and stern fire marshal, could have had a sense of humor?

"Except I'm not running a business." She wiggled her eyebrows at him. "See? I do know a few things about fire codes."

"Details, Olive, details."

She had never liked her name. Kids at school—the same ones that had made her feel left out for being a foster child—would often make fun of her. They'd call her Olive Oyl, teasing her about Popeye, among other things. Not to mention all the teachers who insisted on calling her Olivia no matter how many times she corrected them. But when her name fell from Cal's lips, her tummy did all sorts of melty, fluttery things.

She sneezed as dust flew when he yanked open a stubborn drawer. The musty smell was starting to bother her sinuses. A thorough cleaning needed to go on her project list.

"Aha!" He pulled a small blue box out of the drawer. "I think we hit the jackpot."

He opened it and grinned at her. "Replacement fuses."

"W-will you show me how to replace one?" She wanted to learn how to do this herself—so she wouldn't have to rely on her too-handsome neighbor in the future.

"Of course. Follow me. The most important thing

to remember is to use the right amperage fuse. Otherwise, it's as simple as changing a light bulb."

He showed her the fuses, and the part that screwed in did resemble a miniature light bulb.

"These are fifteen amps so you're safe." He pointed the flashlight above the fuse box to the wires running in and out of it. "Looks like twelve-gauge, which would support twenty amps. But these," he said, holding up the package, "are fifteen and we'll use that to be on the safe side."

"What would happen if I used the twenty-amp ones?" She held up a hand before he could answer. "Let me guess…it's a fire hazard. What do I win for getting the right answer?"

He reached out and touched the tip of his finger to the end of her nose. "Miss Smarty Pants."

She swallowed as her gaze caught his and they were silent for a moment.

He blinked first, staring down at the fuses between them, and she told herself she wasn't disappointed. Nope. Not at all. She cleared her throat. "Why are they made of glass?"

"So we can see which one is bad. They're not marked." He pointed to the row of fuses.

He was right. Changing the fuse was just a matter of unscrewing the bad one and replacing it with a good one.

"Thanks for the help," she told him once he'd finished.

"You're welcome." He closed the electrical panel. "My advice would be to get this replaced with circuit breakers."

Seeing dollar signs, she sighed. She'd known she'd have to invest some money in her new home, but she couldn't afford to rewire the whole house if it needed it. Maybe just this expense? She asked, "How about if I don't use the microwave and the electric teakettle at the same time?"

"As a temporary fix, but you really should get the electrical updated. I know some guys who might be able to help." He frowned. "What?"

"Has anything ever ended well that started with 'I know some guys'?" she asked lightly.

He laughed. "You might have a point, but these guys are fully bonded and licensed electricians. They wouldn't gouge you."

"I guess I could get a quote. At least then I'll know what I'm facing."

"I'll get the information for you. Let them know I referred you."

"I will. Thanks." She climbed the stairs, secretly glad to be leaving the basement behind.

"I thought you said you'd already eaten?"

"What?"

He pointed to the microwave. "Looks like you were heating up some supper."

"Oh, well… I…" She felt annoyed at her stuttering

but couldn't seem to come up with a more coherent answer to his gentle prying.

"It's okay. I wouldn't have accepted my invitation, either. I'm sorry for being so disingenuous."

She shook her head. "I shouldn't have lied. I'm sorry. I just…" What was she supposed to say? She wasn't sure she could resist his charms.

"This smells awesome. What is it?" Cal did his best to pivot the conversation to something—anything—that didn't point out just how keen to get away from him Olive seemed to be. He'd wanted to share a pizza with her, and she'd shot him down. Smart woman, really.

"Nothing fancy, just leftover chicken cacciatore. Would you like some?"

"I don't want to take your supper."

"I have plenty more. You'd be helping me out. The recipe made a lot and I'll be eating the leftovers until I won't be able to stand the thought of more."

"Are you sure?"

"Positive, but what happened to your pizza?"

"The smell of your cooking can't compete with cold pizza zapped in the microwave."

"There are better ways of reheating pizza leftovers," she said.

"If it involves turning on the oven, forget it. Takes too long."

"Believe it or not, it doesn't involve an oven or a

microwave," Olive told him. "Remind me to show you sometime."

"I will."

After a morning spent trapped at her desk filling out assessment reports, Olive left her office to join the residents in one of the common sitting areas. Mingling with the seniors she worked with was an enjoyable aspect of her job. Certainly more fun than filling out paperwork. Some of the women were seated at the tables in groups of four playing bridge. It had been her idea to bring someone in last week to teach the rudiments of the game. Looked like her idea was a success. She flashed back to the previous night, and warm memories of sharing a meal at her kitchen table with Cal floated through her mind.

Feeling a smile tug at her lips, Olive slipped into the empty seat next to Edna Mason, who was seated by herself, just watching the others. Olive knew she wasn't supposed to play favorites—and for the most part she didn't—but something about Edna reached out to her. Was it because she noticed the woman often held herself back from the others, content to sit and observe? Olive recognized the behavior. It reminded her all too much of the way she'd behaved in school…and the way she might be behaving now in Loon Lake if she hadn't met Ellie, Meg and their friends. *And Cal*, she added silently.

"Good morning, Edna. Couldn't you find a bridge partner?"

Edna reached over and patted a bony hand on Olive's thigh. "Don't worry about me, deary. I'm content to sit and watch the others. I think you understand, don't you, dear?"

Olive frowned. Was she that transparent, especially to an elderly woman she didn't know all that well? Before she could respond, Edna was talking again.

"It's my understanding that you spent some of your formative years in foster care."

Olive nodded. She should've known people in town were likely to gossip about her, especially since she was new to town. It wasn't as if she was ashamed of it, but at the same time, she didn't like to be labeled. "From the time I turned eleven."

Edna took Olive's hand and gently squeezed. "What happened? Or don't you want to talk about it?"

"My parents were killed by a drunk driver and they didn't have any close relatives, at least none that wanted to take responsibility for me." She blinked back the stinging in her eyes. What was wrong with her? She'd accepted her situation years ago and moved on. Or hadn't she?

"I hope you were in good places. My Norm and I tried our best to make sure all our children felt safe and welcome."

"You fostered?"

Edna nodded. "I had been in and out of the system as a child and when we couldn't have any of our own, we decided to foster. Ended up permanently adopting three of our placements. But tell me about you."

"I didn't find a permanent placement, but I did okay after a few false starts. Some of that was probably my fault. I wasn't an easy adolescent."

"Oh, honey, don't say that. You weren't to blame for any of it."

"I have to take responsibility for my behavior. I was very introverted and didn't come across well when prospective adoptive parents would take me on outings. Not that I can blame them. Who wants to adopt a child who hangs back, doesn't smile, or speaks in monosyllables?" She had worked hard to come out of her shell in adulthood, even if it was too late for her childhood self.

Edna leaned over and pulled Olive in for a hug. "I wish you'd been placed with us."

"Me, too," Olive said. "Now, how about we find you a bridge partner?"

Cal pulled his official fire department SUV into the lot at Sunshine Gardens Senior Living Center, Loon Lake's skilled nursing facility. He bypassed the impressive porte cochere, with its white Craftsman-style tapered columns and stone facade, to park in an area designated for visitors.

He pointed his key fob over his shoulder and locked the vehicle as he crossed the parking lot. The one-story building was new but had been given a timeless feel with Craftsman architectural features, like the low-pitched triangular roof and wood siding painted in an earthy green. This building was as basic as Olive's Victorian was fussy.

Why did he have to think about her in a familiar way? Sure, they'd had a nice dinner together, and he was here to meet her, but he didn't have feelings for her. He blamed Liam and his outlandish claim that he was going to fall in love. So why did his mind go straight to Olive?

He entered the building through the glass double doors. Straight ahead was a sign-in desk with a vase containing what appeared to be one of those bouquets sold in supermarkets. He'd bought enough of those when he went to visit his nana. Next to the flowers was an industrial-size pump bottle of hand sanitizer, a reminder that this was a medical facility, despite the homey common area with chairs, couches and small tables off to the left.

A woman stood behind the reception desk with her back to him, but there was no mistaking that tumbled mass of golden curls. He frowned when she turned around, taking a stumbling step before stopping in midstride. His heart stuttered when she did that smile that lit up her entire face like a beacon. Damn, but he should've gathered his wits before facing her. Yeah, like that was possible. She had a tendency to scatter them by just looking at him.

"Hello, Fire Marshal Pope," she said sweetly. "Have you come to harass me at work, too?"

Maybe this hadn't been such a good idea. He started to think up plausible excuses for his visit but spotted the teasing sparkle in her eyes. "I came to invite you out to lunch."

She scrunched up her face. "Lunch? With you? Now?"

He couldn't help grinning, despite the tensing in his gut. She made it sound like he'd asked her to go skinny-dipping in the fountain on the green. Not that he'd mind doing that with her some other time. "Yeah, you know, that meal you eat between breakfast and supper."

She glanced at her watch. "It *is* getting close to lunchtime."

"So does this mean you'll go with me?"

She shrugged. "Sure. Let me get my purse and tell someone I'm leaving for a bit."

Not exactly a ringing endorsement, but she'd agreed and that was good enough for him. He watched her walk into one of the offices located beyond the reception desk. Again, he asked himself why he was bothering. He'd told himself it was because he wanted to be on good terms with her because they shared the same set of friends. He didn't want any lingering animosity between them to spill over when they got together as a group. That was his story, and he was sticking to it.

"Do you want me to take my own car and follow you?" she asked as she followed him through the double doors to the parking lot.

"You don't want to ride with me?" He did not sound disappointed to his own ears. Nope. Not at all.

"Oh, no, I didn't mean it like that." She reached over and laid her hand on his arm, sending a frisson of sensation up his tricep. "I just thought that way you wouldn't have to bring me back here."

He didn't respond but saw the way her eyes lit up when she spotted his fire department SUV. He couldn't help puffing his chest out a bit. Sure, it made him feel a bit foolish to be so proud to have apparently impressed her. But he couldn't control his reaction. "And miss a chance to ride in my official vehicle?"

"Does it have a siren?" she said with a slight laugh. Her hand was still on his arm, and she squeezed it a bit, making his heart pound.

"Of course." He grinned. *What is with you, Pope? You're not a teenager trying to impress your date with a cool car. Hell, this wasn't even a date. Nope. Not a date. Not even a lunch date. Just two casual acquaintances...out together. In public.*

She glanced at the red-and-white vehicle and then back to him, a slight pout forming. "But you can only use the lights and siren on official business?"

"We'll see how much trouble you give me."

She laughed. "You probably think I'm acting like some teenybopper excited about riding in the hot guy's cool car. Or a toddler, getting worked up about checking out the fire truck with the siren."

Hot guy? Is that what she thought? Not a date, he reminded himself.

Hurrying to the passenger side, he opened the door for her. She settled into the seat, looked up and thanked him. He shut it with a nod. They were casual friends having lunch, but that didn't mean he should abandon his manners.

He slipped behind the wheel and they headed toward the center of town.

"Are you enjoying small-town life?" he asked as the town green, with its large white gazebo, came into view.

"Yes, although I admit it's a bit unsettling to have people act like they know me when I haven't a clue who they are."

"It's because of the contest."

She huffed out a laugh. "I guess I was a bit slow on the uptake because it spooked me the first few times people approached me."

He suspected she tended to be on the shy side and hoped others weren't too invasive.

It hadn't reached noon yet, so he was able to find a parking spot in front of Aunt Polly's, Loon Lake's most popular local restaurant for breakfast and lunch.

He shut off the engine and half turned in the driver's seat to look at her. "I hope this place is okay with you."

"Absolutely. Everyone has been telling me I needed to try it." She turned her head to look at him. "I'm glad to be here but still not sure why you asked me to join you."

Frankly, he wasn't, either. It had seemed like a good idea in the shower that morning. Part apology for his attitude yesterday toward her cochairing the committee and part—and he wasn't sure he really wanted to admit this to himself—that he wanted to spend time with her.

"I thought we could discuss our plans for the fundraiser." That was the excuse he was most comfortable with.

Her face lit up. "So you mean you're going to take your committee duties seriously?"

His head jerked back. "Do I detect an insult, Ms. Downing?"

She blushed and he noticed a light sprinkling of freckles across the bridge of her nose. Intriguing. How had he not paid any attention to them before? When he'd almost kissed her at her house, the lights had been dim, he realized. That was why he had not seen them previously.

"Have you gotten some sun lately?" he asked. That might explain the freckles. He remembered

Meg complaining about getting more freckles after exposure to the great outdoors.

"Why?" She raised a hand to her face.

"Looks like you've got some fresh freckles," he said, gently touching the bridge of her nose and lightly tracing across the top of her cheek.

She frowned. "I didn't use concealer this morning. I was in too much of a hurry."

"Concealer? What's that? Some sort of makeup, I assume. Why would you want to conceal them?"

She gave him a look. "Because they're freckles and I'm not ten years old."

He reached out and touched the end of her nose. "I like them."

Her big, light brown eyes widened. "You do?"

"Why so surprised?"

She shrugged. "I don't know. I guess..."

He leaned over before he lost his nerve and pressed his lips to hers. Just a light peck. Not romantic or passionate, just friendly. He pulled back and their gazes collided. He had a feeling her surprise was mirrored on his own face.

He cleared his throat, as did she. Damn, but that was supposed to be a nonromantic gesture. So why was his heart pounding as if he was about to jump from the helicopter into a battle zone?

It was a stupid move and yet he didn't regret doing it. He probably should, but he didn't.

"Well..."

"Well, I…"

He fisted his hand around his keys, then blurted out awkwardly, "We probably should go inside if we want to beat the lunch rush."

She nodded, as if relieved he'd found a way to move the conversation forward. "Good idea."

Cal jumped out and started toward the passenger side, but she had already gotten out and was shutting the door.

They entered the restaurant and warm air carried the scents of coffee, cinnamon and bacon grease. Directly across from the entrance was a long counter with stools, but only three were occupied by customers. Half a dozen booths lined up along the front windows with currently unoccupied tables between the counter and the booths.

A stout blonde waitress stood behind the counter pouring coffee from a glass pot into the mugs of those seated at the counter. She looked up and smiled. "As I live and breathe, it's Cal Pope. Haven't seen you in ages. Where have you been hiding? You haven't been dining at the competition, have you?"

"Aw, Trudi, you should know by now no one can compete with you."

"You just remember that," she said and inclined her head at a vacant booth. "You two have a seat and I'll be right with you."

The customers seated at the counter turned to look when the waitress mentioned Cal having a companion. Two men dressed in shirts with cable-company logos smiled and nodded. A man Cal recognized as the bank manager, Bruce Sterling, greeted Olive by name and she gave the man her full-wattage smile in return.

Cal frowned as he recalled the fortysomething branch manager was recently divorced. Not that he was jealous or anything, but he'd heard some talk of extramarital affairs causing the divorce. He wouldn't want to see Olive hurt.

But it wasn't any of his business. This wasn't even a date, despite the fact he'd just kissed his "lunch partner." He was just making nice so as not to upset Ellie or Liam. He should be relieved to see Olive interested in another eligible man. Right? Because he certainly wasn't interested in settling down and helping her fill that house with kids and dogs. He was already settled and—

"Cal? Is this booth okay with you?"

He blinked and met Olive's quizzical gaze. Damn. He needed to keep his head in the game when he was with her. He cleared his throat but his "sure" still came out rough.

Trudi sauntered over after they'd slipped into the red vinyl booth. She put two pebbled plastic tumblers with ice water on the table, along with dog-eared menus. "Have a look and I'll be back."

"I'm so happy you asked me to lunch."

Cal's head snapped up from the menu he was pretending to read. Did she think this was more than an attempt to be friends? Damn. How was he going to explain his reasons for inviting her? But before he could think of a response she continued. "Liam hinted that you might be window dressing when it came to the committee."

His shoulders sagged with relief. "I'll deal with McBride later, but let's get one thing straight. I intend to pull my weight on this committee."

"I'm glad," she said.

The smile she gave him poked at his conscience. Before he could lose his nerve, he said, "I also want to say that I think you may have overheard something I hadn't meant you to hear and I'm sorry."

Olive's eyes widened. "I assume you're referring to the cookout."

He nodded. "I hope you'll accept my apology."

Something he couldn't read flickered over her face. "Of course. I—"

"So, what can I get for you two?" Trudi returned with her order pad and pencil at the ready. She grinned. "Should I get a milkshake with two straws for the lovebirds?"

Olive turned red and Cal stammered a denial. They were not on a date, he told Trudi firmly, and each of them quietly ordered their meals. But as Trudi walked off, the memory of kissing Olive, and the waitress picturing them as a couple, weighed on him.

Another reason not to get involved with his lovely neighbor. Surely his friends would be all over him, asking when they were taking it to the next level. He might be happy for his pals who had found love and happiness. But that was never going to be him.

Olive stood at her kitchen sink and turned on the tap to fill a spray bottle with water. The ancient pipes groaned as she shut off the faucet. Maybe she needed to ask Cal if he knew some plumbers, too.

The thought of Cal made her pause. It had been two days since their lunch...date? Was that what it had been? Their waitress had seemed to think so. And yesterday, when she'd gone to the bank to sign some paperwork, the manager, Bruce Sterling, said he would have mentioned the papers when he saw her but hadn't wanted to interrupt her date.

She screwed the top back onto the spray bottle. Bruce had obviously been fishing for more information by mentioning her lunch with Cal. She'd even started to deny that it had been a date, but had stopped before the words had escaped. Why?

The question nagged at her as she went outside to spritz the Boston ferns hanging between the posts on the front porch.

"Veranda," she said, remembering Cal calling it that. She liked that word, too. And she liked Cal. A little too much. Was that why she hadn't corrected Bruce's assumption?

As if her thoughts had conjured him up, Cal pulled his pickup into her driveway.

He exited the truck, raised his hand in greeting and went to the back of his truck. He reached in, then straightened up and came toward her with a pot of red and yellow gerbera daisies.

He bounced up the five steps and held out the flowers.

"Oh, my. Those are so pretty. But I don't understand. What are they for?"

"They're, uh—" he cleared his throat "—for you."

"Thank you," she said, smiling. "That's so sweet."

"I stopped by the garden center and saw those. They reminded me of you."

"Well, thank you so much, but I still don't understand why you felt compelled to bring me flowers."

"As a proper apology for what I said at the cookout."

"I thought you already apologized. When we went to lunch."

"That was hardly an apology." He shook his head. "That was a bunch of passive-aggressive…uh, crap. A sincere apology is me being sorry I said it. Not that you heard it."

"That's what I get for eavesdropping."

He shook his head. "I doubt you heard it on purpose. I can't imagine you'd stoop to that."

"No, but if I had made my presence known, perhaps I wouldn't have heard something I now wish I hadn't."

"I'm sorry I said it. I hope you'll accept my apology."

"And the daisies?"

"The flowers are yours, even if you don't accept the apology."

"Thank you for both. Consider yourself forgiven. Would you like to come in?" She laughed. "Said the spider to the fly."

"If the spider is as pretty as you, I think the fly would go happily."

"Be careful or I might get the wrong idea."

"Can't have that."

"Friends?"

"Friends."

"Would you like to come in? I made some tropical tea."

He tilted his head to the side. "Tropical tea?"

She placed the pot and spray bottle on the wicker side table she'd spray-painted a milky white. She smiled at how the cheerful flowers brightened the spot.

Smile still in place, she glanced up at him. "It's nothing fancy. Just an Arnold Palmer with a spritz of coconut syrup."

He returned her smile. "Sounds delicious."

"It is," she said and frowned as a thought occurred to her. "It's nonalcoholic."

"That's only because you haven't put any booze into it yet," he said and winked.

"Oh. I'm not sure I have anything that—"

"I'm just messing with you, Olive." He put his hand on her arm.

She swallowed hard as the warmth from his fingers seeped into her skin. If anyone had asked if she enjoyed being teased, she would have set them straight with a resounding no. And yet, when Cal teased her it felt different. It *was* different. Behind his teasing was gentle affection, a shared joke. Whatever it was, she quite liked it. "Does that mean you'd like to come in for a nonalcoholic cocktail?"

"I would. Thanks." He dropped his hand, but his smile stayed firmly in place.

Cal blamed her smile. That lift of her lips, the light in her eyes, the way her cheeks bloomed; it all worked to rob him of his common sense. He *knew* this couldn't go anywhere, but when she smiled, he had trouble remembering why. Following her into the house, he admired her backside. He should feel guilty for his thoughts. But no matter how hard he tried, he couldn't dredge up an appropriate amount of shame.

In the kitchen, he took a seat at the table while she got the ingredients out of the refrigerator. Did she have any idea what she did to him, the confusion she created?

He watched her putter around her kitchen and

wished he could place the blame on her physical qualities for the emotional turmoil she created within him. But this wasn't simple lust. He could deal with that. No, this was more. Because of that tenderheartedness of hers, he felt a part of himself being drawn in, even opening up to her despite—or maybe because of—her ability to scrape against parts of him that were raw.

And yet instead of fleeing, here he was sitting in her kitchen drinking tea.

Chapter Six

Cal cursed under his breath as he exited his truck after work a few days later. He spied Olive, bent over the trunk of her car and apparently trying to lift something heavy.

Mind your own business, he cautioned himself, but she was still struggling with whatever she was trying to remove from her car.

Muttering a curse, he checked the street for cars and sprinted across. What was it about her that made him want to be there for her? He would have sworn he wasn't the type to rescue damsels in distress. In his mind, both his time in the air force and with the fire department were different from helping a woman with a blown fuse and one who walked into a spiderweb.

"Wait. Let me help with that," he said as he approached despite enjoying the view of her rear as she bent over the trunk as he walked up her driveway. He thought he heard her chatting away. Was she talking to herself or to someone else on the Bluetooth on her phone? *Another guy?* He chastised himself for the jealousy flaring up in him at the thought.

She bobbled the item and dropped it back into the trunk. Whirling around, she put her hands on her hips and blushed. "You startled me."

"I didn't exactly sneak up on you," he pointed out. "Didn't you hear me coming? These size twelves aren't exactly stealthy."

"If you must know, my attention was on the plants. I was…uh, I was talking to them." She pulled her lower lip between her teeth, looking as if she regretted letting that bit of information slip.

Cal swallowed his groan. What he wouldn't give to put his mouth over that lip and pull it into his mouth once again. He shifted his weight and moved a leg slightly forward.

"Talking to them?" he repeated and chuckled.

She scowled at him, and he scolded himself for acting like such a jerk. Why did he always put his foot in his mouth with her? He knew he'd hurt her feelings by laughing at her plans for the B and B soon after being introduced. In his defense, he didn't think she could possibly be serious. But she had been, and although he'd apologized, he still felt bad and wished he'd offered more of an apology. Only now that time had passed, it would be awkward to bring it up. So, he'd let it lie. Helping her with her renovations, either by doing the work he was capable of or steering her toward pros when he couldn't, might be a good way of making amends.

It was also getting harder and harder to remember his reasons for keeping his distance from her. He needed to keep their conversations light or run the risk of embarrassment. His libido had a mind of its own around Olive. He'd even thought about getting out of the dating rut he'd been in since meeting her. He normally didn't go this long without female companionship. And yet, each time he'd thought about calling someone, he found excuses not to. Strange.

"Do you have a problem with me talking to my plants?"

Her question brought him out of his thoughts. Remembering that he wanted to keep things light, he shook his head. "Not unless they start answering you back."

She surprised him by laughing. "You'll be the first to know if they do. I promise."

He grinned, grateful she hadn't taken offense. "We might not need that fundraiser if they do. We could just charge admission for Olive's talking plants."

He strolled over to her open trunk, expecting to see flowering plants.

"Umm… Olive?" Cal asked curiously.

"Yes?"

"Where did you get these?"

"The nursery on the other side of town. I believe it's called Connor's. Why?"

He glanced at what she was referring to as plants. They were more brown than green, and calling them "wilted" was putting it mildly. What the...? As far as he was concerned, they were about as appealing as roadkill. "Were they piled next to that big blue receptacle out behind the place?"

"You mean the trash? No, they weren't in the trash, although I bought them out of a marked-down bin."

"If you didn't get them for free, then you paid too much," he told her. "What possessed you to buy these?"

"I bought them because no one else wanted them." She said it as if it made perfect sense.

Cal shook his head at her logic. Was she blind or that tenderhearted? He hated the thought of people taking advantage of her or hurting her. Like himself? He pushed aside those thoughts to concentrate on the present. "I can clearly see why no one else wanted them."

"I felt sorry for them. I know what it's like to never get chosen."

Cal's chest tightened at her words, and he had trouble drawing in air. He could all too easily picture the hopeful child she must have been. The urge to draw her into his embrace and promise she'd never have to feel like that again was too great. He needed to step back from these feelings before he did something stupid, like follow his instincts.

What had her childhood been like? He knew from comments Ellie had made that Olive had spent some years in foster care. Like him, his new neighbor obviously hadn't had an easy time of it. But now wasn't the time to start taking trips down memory lane.

Yeah, keeping things light seemed to work best when it came to controlling his libido. He reached into the trunk and hoisted the flat of wilted and yellowed plants. "In the life they had prior to this one, what were they?"

"Gerbera daisies. Like the ones you brought me. They have such beautiful flowers." Her face lit up and her cheeks exploded when she smiled, reminding him of flowers. Ones that were alive and flourishing.

He glanced down at the flat in his arms. "I'll take your word for it."

"I'll bring them back to life. You'll see."

"Uh-huh." He didn't doubt her dedication or her ability to nurture these poor plants. Shifting his burden, he grunted. Not from exertion but because he believed she could revive them. Look at what she was doing to him! Instead of calling her out on her choice of plants, he was helping her. "Where do you want them?"

"Over there by the garden statuary."

"Statuary? Is that what you're calling those things? I thought they were gnomes. Like in that commercial for that travel service."

She frowned. "The way you say that I get the feeling you think my gnomes are tacky?"

"Don't go putting words in my mouth." No. *Put your tongue or that lower lip you like to worry in my mouth.* What was he doing, steering things back into dangerous territory? He'd lightened things up so he could control his response to her. He set down the flowers.

"Are you the garden police now?" She shot him a side-eye. "Pointing out fire codes isn't good enough?"

He held up his hands palms out. "I mean no disrespect to your gnomes. They're very…uh, colorful."

She narrowed her eyes, but her lips were twitching, as if a smile was about to burst forth. "And colorful is code for…?"

"Something that's brightly colored." He glanced across the yard and motioned toward the corner, where a carved cat statue stood. "Did the cat do something to force his ouster from the group?"

She slowly shook her head, the corners of her mouth turned down. "Max is buried there."

"Max?"

She blinked several times and nodded. "He was my cat."

"Oh, God. I shouldn't have teased you about it."

Those beautiful golden eyes of hers were shiny.

Those could only be tears. He had an urge that had nothing to do with her attractiveness or his desire for her. She had obviously cared a whole lot about this pet, which was making him want to pull her into his arms and comfort her. And wanting something was a lot more dangerous than fantasizing about biting her lower lip, then soothing the sting with his tongue, and letting his hands rove over her body. Wanting to comfort her was delving into very different territory for him, territory he generally stayed out of. As he was going to do this time.

She shrugged, a small, sad gesture. "It's okay."

Without conscious thought, he reached out and pulled her closer. He hugged her close and briefly rested his chin on the top of her head. Her hair smelled like lavender, too.

"I'm sorry about your cat," he said and rubbed her back.

All the while he held her, he silently urged her to step away because Lord knew he suddenly didn't have the strength. Instead of stepping back, she melted against him, accepting the comfort he offered.

What happened to that promise he'd made not to do this? He wasn't that guy, and yet here he was giving her back soothing rubs. And he definitely wasn't a soothing-back-rubs kind of guy. At least he hadn't been for any other woman.

She sniffed and he went totally still, all his muscles

froze. Oh, God. Not tears. He didn't think he could handle tears. He could handle her laugh. Her smile. Well, at least he had a handle on how he could deal with that bright grin. But he had no shield against her tears. His spontaneous reaction must have galvanized her into action, because she pulled back. And he dropped his arms. Her pulling away first eased some of his guilt.

She blinked and smiled. "Thanks. I had him fifteen years and they speculate he was at least three years old when I rescued him, so he had a good long life."

"But you still miss him?" He drew his eyebrows together as he studied her. He'd had a dog as a child—at least for a time—so he knew how she must be hurting at the loss.

"The house doesn't feel the same without him."

"Why don't you adopt another one?" He glanced up at the house. "You certainly have room."

"I'd like to…" She gnawed on her lower lip again but this time he wanted to soothe her, not kiss her.

"But?"

She lifted her shoulder in a half-hearted shrug. "It feels weird…like I'm replacing him. I feel guilty every time I think about it."

"I'm sure he wouldn't want you to not ever have another cat. Sounds like you gave him a good long life."

She smiled. "I'm not sure how he'd feel about me getting another cat. Maybe someday."

"I never had a cat, but I had a dog as a kid. His name was Rufus."

She laid her hand on his arm. "What happened?"

"We had to move when I was fifteen and had to surrender him." He hadn't told anyone how much it hurt to lose his pet after his dad leaving meant his mom could no longer afford to stay in their house. He felt guilty for blaming his mother for that years ago, but his resentment still lingered. Oh, sure, his mom had been there physically, but she'd checked out emotionally from everything, even parenting. He'd had to pretty much take care of himself from then on. She went through the motions, but he'd never felt he'd gotten his mother back. She'd died of an aneurysm during his time in the air force, so any hopes of a happy ending were gone. All he could do was mourn for the loss of what might have been.

"I'm so sorry. That must've been so painful for you."

He shrugged, already regretting sharing with her. Her genuine concern made his chest ache. "It was twenty years ago."

"Time doesn't matter for things like that," she told him, her golden eyes full of sympathy.

He wanted to shrug off her hand but didn't. He wanted to brush off her concern and couldn't. Why did her expressing sympathy for something that happened so long ago mean so much?

"You never got another one?" Olive asked.

"We couldn't," he said. "And then when I joined the air force it wasn't possible."

"But you've been out of the military for some time, haven't you?"

"Never wanted the hassle." At least that's what he told himself, but he'd gotten good at making excuses. He just couldn't stand the thought of opening himself up for any more eventual pain because chances were a dog or cat would not outlive him.

"I grieve for my loss," Olive told him, "but I wouldn't trade those years for anything."

"You can't tell me it was worth the pain."

"Oh, but it was. Absolutely. He filled up those fifteen years. I still catch myself searching for him. He was very good at hide-and-seek." She laughed when Cal raised a skeptical eyebrow. "He liked to find places to hide and take a nap. As small as many of the apartments I've lived in were, he got very creative in finding places. He scared me a couple of times. I was afraid he'd gotten out somehow."

"Cats don't come when you call?" he joked.

"Some might, but not this one." She chuckled, her eyes glowing. "But I had a trick or two up my sleeve. He couldn't resist the sound of the can opener. Of course, I'd feel guilty for tricking him and would invariably end up opening a can of tuna. The water from the can was an extraspecial treat." She sighed. "I ended up eating a lot of tuna sandwiches."

"You do realize he was getting rewarded for hiding?" he said drily.

"Yeah, but it beat that sick feeling in my stomach when I couldn't find him."

"You're very softhearted."

"And you think that's a bad thing?"

"No, but I do worry that you're going to get that heart broken."

Was he referring to himself and the fact he'd probably hurt her if they became involved? And wasn't that a tad bit arrogant, thinking he wielded the power to break a woman's heart?

"It's happened in the past and I survived."

"You thinking what I'm thinking?"

"We are if you now have a certain song stuck in your head."

He laughed. "Wasn't that before your time?"

"Yours, too."

"So how come you know it?"

"Probably the same way you do. That handwashing PSA Gloria Gaynor did."

"I don't remember but you're probably right."

Olive invited him inside for lunch and made him a sandwich. He gave the meal—four precisely cut pieces on his plate—a pointed look and then raised his gaze to her. "Thanks?"

"Sorry. Force of habit. Here, I didn't cut mine yet."

She leaned over his shoulder, giving him a whiff of her fresh scent.

He circled her wrist with his hand before she could remove the plate. "It's fine. My mom used to do that."

His mother had done a dozen little things like that before life had changed. Once again, Olive gave him back memories of a happier time in his life, even though his attraction to her made it clear he didn't see her in a familial way in the least. It wasn't something she'd set out to do but the result was the same. He was forced to accept that there was something about her that had him facing his past…and not just concentrating on the bad stuff. And he was enjoying it.

She sighed. "Yeah, it's one of the things I remember about my mom, too. I guess that's why I do it."

"How old were you when you lost your parents?"

"Eleven."

"That must have been tough." *That's all you can say?* he asked himself. *Of course, it was tough for her. That's a given.*

"Yeah. I ended up in foster care. My parents were wonderful people but neither one was close to any of their relatives. They had some distant ones but that's about it."

"There was no one to take you in?"

"No. They found some cousins, but they weren't interested in taking in an orphan that they had never even met." His heart ached for her. At least he'd had his mom after his dad had left. Olive had had no one. And she was still open to making friends and starting over again? His admiration for her grew leaps and bounds in an instant.

"Not all the placements were bad. Most of the people were really decent, but it wasn't the same as having your own biological family."

"I can't imagine what that must have been like, to suddenly be thrust into that situation." No wonder she had so much empathy for things others might overlook or consider unworthy of her time or consideration. She must have been disregarded quite a bit as a kid.

"I was at an awkward age, and I confess that after my parents died, I had a lot of unresolved anger."

"But you seem to have resolved it," he offered. *Whereas I haven't even gotten past my dad leaving me. And I* still *had one parent...*

"Yeah, I was lucky to get some counseling but that, too, made some people nervous. If I needed counseling, though, a lot of the couples were concerned with my state of mind. Worrying that I was somehow damaged or possibly dangerous."

"Well, I gotta say you turned into one wonderful human being, despite—or because of—your past." Maybe if he had confronted his demons instead of burying them, he might deserve someone like Olive. As it was, though, he was in awe of her...and knew he wasn't worthy of his new neighbor.

Chapter Seven

Olive opened the lid of the slow cooker and took a whiff of what was inside. She was grateful that she'd taken the time to get her supper going before she'd left for work. Even if it meant dragging out of bed earlier than usual that morning…and dragging herself away from dreams of kissing Cal again, talking endlessly about their lives, delving into his own past and not just hers. It had been two days since they'd spent that time together and she was still replaying it in her mind…and in her dreams.

She returned the lid to the slow cooker. Judging by how much the recipe made, she'd have leftovers for the rest of the week. Enough for lunch and another dinner. But just because she lived alone didn't mean she couldn't have a hearty meal every once in a while.

The doorbell chimed so she put the cover back on the Crock-Pot and adjusted the cooking temperature to warm. She wiped her hands on a kitchen towel and tossed it on the counter.

At the front door, she glanced out of one of the sidelights and her heart jumped, her pulse beginning to race. It was Cal. He was in his fire-marshal uniform again, but his slightly disheveled appearance reminded her of the day he'd brought the ice cream to Camp Life Launch, making her smile. His white shirt was dirty and his hair was even more mussed than usual. Each time she saw him like that, she wanted to run her hands through all that silky darkness.

"Olive?" he called through the door.

Quit standing here just gawking at him, she admonished herself. *If you can see him, he can surely see you.* That's when she noticed it looked as though he was carrying something in each hand pressed close to his chest. She pulled open the door.

Cal stood there, a pair of tabby kittens nestled close to his chest, one on each side. How was it that she didn't melt into a puddle right then and there? It was like her very own firefighter calendar come to life and Cal was Mr. May. Ha! More like January through December.

She could barely believe her eyes. The cats he was carrying looked quite young, possibly eight to twelve weeks old. They were black and gray, nearly identical except one had blue eyes and the other had green eyes.

"Oh, my goodness, they're adorable. Are they yours?" She couldn't help gushing. What was he doing with them, and more importantly why was he bringing them to her? "Where did you get them?"

"I was doing an inspection out at the refreshment stand at the abandoned drive-in movie theater. I heard noises and went to check it out and…*mmmfff.*"

One of the kittens began batting at his face, one tiny paw swiping at his lips. She couldn't help laughing at its antics. No wonder he looked so disheveled, if he'd been dealing with them for any amount of time.

"Here." She took pity on him and swung the door wider. "Come on in. Were these little guys there by themselves?"

He stepped inside and shifted the kittens. They mewled and tried to climb on his shoulder. He winced as one dug its claws into his chest.

"Here, let me take one." She reached out, glancing at him as she asked, "If that's okay with you?"

Color stained his cheeks and he handed one over to her. "That's actually why I'm here. You were a cat owner, so I assumed you'd know what to do with these two. I didn't have a clue after I found them."

One kitten crawled to her shoulder and cuddled against her neck with a rusty, purring sound. Having that warm ball of fluff snuggled against her made her eyes sting and she had to blink several times. She refused to embarrass herself in front of Cal by crying over a kitten. A kitten that wasn't even hers.

"Max was already an adult when I adopted him, though. These guys look pretty young. You didn't see a mother cat around? Although the way this little guy is snuggling, they're not feral. They are accustomed to people handling them."

He nodded. "That's what Velma said."

"Velma?" Thoughts began racing through her mind. Who was she and what was Cal doing with her? Was he dating her? And if he was, what business was it of hers?

"Velma Sawyer. She lives across the street from the former drive-in. It's on the other side of town, closer to the beach side of the lake. I stopped at her place to see if she knew anything about these little guys. She didn't but said the drive-in is a dumping ground for unwanted animals."

"That's terrible. How can people be so cruel?" Her throat thickened and she had to swallow several times to try to get past the closure to speak again. "Are you sure you didn't see a momma cat around?"

"They seemed to be alone, but just in case I put them in a box so they couldn't wander off and get hurt. That place isn't safe for people let alone curious kittens. I—I had a teddy bear in the SUV, so I put that in there with them." The color in his cheeks darkened and he shuffled his feet.

"A teddy bear?" Did she hear that right? "Why did you have a teddy bear?"

How was she supposed to stay irritated with a guy like that? How was she supposed to guard her heart against a guy who was good with kids, rescued abandoned kittens and just happened to have a teddy bear to give said baby animals? Couple that with those deep-set brown eyes and an untidy mop of dark hair, and she didn't stand a chance.

"Remember when…no, wait that was probably before your time. Anyway, the ladies from the church raised money to buy stuffed animals for the police and fire departments to carry in their official vehicles for calls that involved young children. It helps ease the trauma a bit and gives them something to cling to."

"That was really sweet of you, to think of that for the kittens."

His reply was a grunt. Yeah, it didn't sound as if he appreciated her assessment of his character based on his actions. But for her, sweet was way more dangerous to her well-being than any macho thing he could have done. Of course, she wasn't about to admit that to him. Running into a burning building was his job and that spoke to his character, but personally rescuing kittens while on the job was a personal choice. He could have contacted the local humane society or a vet and let them deal with just another case of abandoned baby creatures, but he didn't. He came to Olive, whom he knew adored cats. To her, that made him a hero.

"So what did you do?" she continued.

"I went back later for them. I figured if there was a mother cat somewhere, that gave her time to come and collect them. But when I got back there was no sign of another cat or even more kittens. I swept through the entire building but didn't see any evidence of another animal. I couldn't just leave them overnight, so I took them."

"What about this Velma person you mentioned?"

"Velma Sawyer. I believe her mother is at Sunshine Gardens. Velma is tall, short gray hair."

"Does she wear plaid flannel shirts?" He nodded and she continued, "Okay. I may have met her when she came to visit her mother at Sunshine Gardens. I remember talking to someone who said she worked at the concession stand when she was in high school. It was my first day and all the names of everyone I met are a bit of a blur."

He pried the kitten away from the front of his shirt. "That's probably her."

"She couldn't take them herself?"

"She said that's how she's ended up with three cats and two dogs." He huffed out a laugh. "She was pretty adamant about not taking them in, even just as fosters."

"I guess I can't blame her. That's a lot of animals."

He sighed and winced as he pried kitten claws off his scalp.

"C'mon into the kitchen. We can put them on the floor in there. I wonder when they last ate."

"I fed them this afternoon."

She smiled at him. "Don't tell me you also carry cat food around with you."

"No. I had planned to stop at the Pic-N-Save, but Liam called and asked for my assistance at a suspected arson site he'd been working for the state. So I went through a fast-food drive-through on the way and bought some chicken nuggets."

"Calvin Pope, I don't believe it! You fed these little ones fast food?" The kitten in her arms lifted its head and mewled at her. "I know, baby, I know."

"Hey, I had to think fast, and they didn't complain. I ate some myself, so why not them?"

She shook her head and he continued, "If it makes you feel any better, I scraped off the breading and gave them just the chicken. Cats are carnivores, so what could it hurt? And it was better than all of us starving while I helped Liam out."

She had to admit that he was right, even if his solution wasn't the ideal one.

"Well, they probably need to eat some real cat food, but I'm afraid I don't have any cat things left over from Max, so I have nothing for them."

"That's okay. I stopped at Pic-N-Save after I called Emily."

"Emily?"

"Dr. Emily Greer, the local vet. I called her and she agreed to wait until I could get to her office. She gave them a cursory exam and pronounced them healthy, and both females. Said to call in the morning to set up an appointment for a more thorough exam."

She nodded, still processing the fact he was on a first-name basis with the petite, twentysomething veterinarian. And why shouldn't he be? They were both adults. She'd put her reaction down to jealousy, except...

Except that wasn't possible. Was it?

He studied her for a beat, then said, "I got a bunch of cat stuff from the Pic-N-Save. It's in my truck."

"So you're keeping them?" She couldn't decide whether to be relieved or disappointed. To be fair, she couldn't expect someone to take on two baby animals suddenly. And Cal clearly wasn't someone to enter into any commitment lightly...if at all.

"Well, I, uh… I thought you might keep them."

"Me? Why me?" Did she want to? She'd told him the joy of those fifteen years with Max had been worth the eventual pain of losing him. Had she been honest with him and with herself?

"I thought maybe you'd be willing to take them. I thought of you when I saw them. You said you missed Max."

"But…"

"You'd be doing me a big favor," he said, his tone cajoling.

"Why don't you take them?"

"I think they need a caring person's touch. They're so young, and they don't have any parents. And you'd be absolved of guilt over replacing Max because I'm practically forcing you to take them."

He grinned and held the kitten up next to his face. "How can you resist?"

"You really know how to play dirty, Pope," she said because she couldn't resist those furry bundles. Or Cal, for that matter.

She'd known all along that at some point she'd be getting another cat. Not a replacement for Max. No, but furry companions, other living, breathing beings to share her space. And thanks to Cal, she was taking the first step in making that dream come true.

Cal watched her with the kittens and knew he'd done a good thing. The smile on her face as she played with the little balls of fur made him grin, too. Any doubts he might have had about whether or not he was doing the right thing vanished.

But he still asked, "So you'll give them a home?"

She looked up from where she was sitting on the kitchen floor with the lively kittens and slowly shook her head at him. "You knew I would. That's why you brought them instead of just calling."

"You mean text. No one calls anymore. Haven't you noticed that?" He rubbed a hand across his mouth.

She gave him an exasperated look. "Don't change the subject. You knew I would be a soft touch. That's why you brought them to me."

"That's only part of it." He hunkered down next to her. "You're caring and kind."

A little too tenderhearted. But maybe that wasn't so bad.

"A true humanitarian," he added with a grin.

She made a noise that indicated skepticism.

He quirked an eyebrow. "Too much?"

"Don't push your luck, Calvin."

Before he could respond or process how he felt hearing his full name from her lips, one of the kittens chomped down on the end of his shoelace and scampered away, pulling the lace along. "Hey, you, come back with that."

He grabbed the kitten, who dropped the aglet, scrunched up her face and meowed. His gaze bounced between Olive and the kitten. She burst out laughing and he joined her.

Giving someone a pet—or two!—was risky. But he'd suspected she'd react favorably. He'd based his decision on the fact she had given him a good feeling. Like he'd placed his trust in the right person.

Cal parked his pickup in his own driveway but didn't go into his house. Instead, he hoisted a box out of his truck bed and headed across the street. Two days had passed since Cal had brought the kittens to Olive. Two days in which he'd kept in touch with her by texting. She'd told him briefly about the comprehensive exam, which included shots and standard deworming meds administered by Dr. Greer. She'd also scheduled for the pair to be spayed.

He'd felt strangely disappointed because he hadn't been able to accompany her. Would he have tagged along? The decision was taken out of his hands when he'd gotten called downstate the next morning. He'd been asked to investigate the origins of a suspicious fire through a reciprocal agreement Loon Lake had with other small towns in the area.

He shifted the box and reached out to ring the bell. He wasn't sure why he felt the need to bring her more supplies for the kittens.

But that's a lie, a voice in his head accused. *You wanted an excuse to come and see her*. The kittens had been that excuse. He glanced around the porch as he waited for her to answer the door. There was a swing at the far end where the porch curved around the tower. A perfect spot to sit and enjoy an evening, maybe wrap his arm around her and kiss her slowly but passionately. But it looked as though the seat part had become detached from the ceiling. He made a mental note to fix it for her. It could also use a coat of paint. He had some left from his own renovations. *When did you start becoming Olive's personal handyman?* he asked himself sardonically.

The door opened and he swung back around. Her hair was scooped back from her face and held in place with one of those fancy rubber-band thingies that women wore. Curls had escaped from it to frame her face. She was dressed casually in faded jeans and a hot-pink T-shirt. She was too casual to be dressed like a fashion model, but her appearance made his pulse pound and heat rush to his neck.

"Hey."

"Hey, yourself."

A crash came from somewhere in the house and she sighed. "You'd better come in. I need to go see what that was."

He stepped over the threshold, adjusted the box and turned to shut the door. Following the sound of her voice, he headed for the back of the house. He found her in the small sitting room off the kitchen.

She was kneeling down next to a small dish and a bunch of wrapped hard candies, which were scattered across the floor. She'd picked up one of the kittens by the scruff of its neck and was holding it in front of her face. "What have I told you about knocking things off the end tables?" she said sharply.

The kitten meowed and batted her paw on Olive's face.

"It's a good thing you're so darn cute," she said and laughed, hugging the animal to her. And his cold heart melted just a little bit, like the smoke heralding the beginning of a fire. Should he keep an eye out for sparks?

He cleared his throat and set the box next to the couch. "Sounds like you're getting along."

A paw crept out from under the couch and swiped at his shoelaces. He hunkered down and reached for the kitten. "Have you decided on names yet?"

"As a matter of fact, I have. The one with the green eyes is Mischief and the blue-eyed one is Mayhem."

He threw his head back and laughed heartily. "Dare I ask?"

"It's exactly as it sounds. I may have been a cat owner, but this is the first time I've ever had kittens. I have a feeling the experience is like suddenly having toddlers in your home. I've been kitten-proofing the place, but they keep finding new things and places I've missed."

"I'm sorry. I had no idea."

She touched his arm. "I'm not complaining. They've brought some real life into the house. I hadn't even realized it was missing until now."

"So you're not looking to get revenge on me?" he joked.

"Maybe at four this morning when Mischief used the comforter to climb up the side of my bed and woke me up."

What he wouldn't have given to have traded

places with the kitten this morning. And that was a sentence he'd never imagined thinking... "Sorry?"

"No, you're not. The last two nights I shut them in the bathroom after I childproofed it, but I felt bad for them, even though they had one another for company."

"You didn't put them back in the bathroom after they woke you up?"

She pointed the kitten's tiny, adorable face at him. "How could I?"

"You're a soft touch."

"Which you know, since you're the one who brought them here, knowing full well you could unload them on me."

He laughed. "You could have said no."

"It would have served you right if I had."

"Is that a timer going off?" He'd heard beeping in the background during their conversation.

"Don't try to change the— Oh! That's my lasagna."

As if on cue, his stomach rumbled. Talk about embarrassing.

"Would you like to stay for supper?"

"Do you have enough?"

"Yeah, I had planned on leftovers," she admitted.

"Well, then I shouldn't..."

"I didn't say I liked having leftovers, just that I was going to have some."

He grinned. "So I should have paid more attention?"

"Yes. Keep up. So you'll stay for supper?"

"Yes, please."

He followed her into the kitchen, picking up a kitten who was trying to trip him. "Which one was the blue-eyed one?"

"Mayhem," she said as she slipped on a pair of oven mitts.

"Is that what you cause?" he asked the animal, who slowly closed one eye, seemingly in response. "Did she just wink at me?"

Olive set the casserole pan on a hot pad on the counter and pulled off the gloves. She bent down and put a loaf of garlic bread in the oven.

Straightening up, she reached over and scratched around Mayhem's ear. "You should feel honored. That's a cat kiss."

He held the kitten in front of his face. "Huh. Am I supposed to wink back?"

"Just open and close your eyes slowly. She might wink back." She pulled plates from the cupboard and set them on the table. "What was in the box?"

"A cat tree." He was still trying to get the kitten to repeat the wink, but she wouldn't. "Maybe it was a fluke."

She set glasses on the table. "Like a baby's first smile is usually— You bought them a cat tree?"

He shrugged, feeling a little sheepish. He stifled the urge to confess he felt partially responsible for them. Who would have thought he'd be "sharing" a pair of kittens with her? "I understand it's…uh, stimulating for indoor cats."

She was staring at him, and he felt warmth rise in his face. He cleared his throat and—

Taking a stumbling step toward him, she threw her arms around him, the kitten smooshed between them.

"Oops," she said and pulled back a little. Petting Mayhem, she apologized.

"I'll be their cool uncle," he said.

Something flickered in her eyes before she blinked and whatever emotion it was disappeared before he could decipher it. But he got the distinct impression he'd disappointed her. Or was he thinking of himself? Cool Uncle Cal was the role he played with his friends' kids, and until Olive, he'd never minded it. Now he wondered if the whole marriage-and-kids path was the right one.

"And I'll probably be that local cat lady." She laughed.

"Hear that?" he asked the kitten. "You've got it made."

She grabbed an oven mitt and pulled the bread out of the oven, filling the room with the fragrant scent of garlic.

He set down the kitten and went to the sink to wash his hands. "Can I help with anything?"

"I've got it covered."

Drying his hands on a towel from the counter, he

watched her set things on the table. Normally, the domestic scene would leave him itching under his skin, but he wasn't getting that.

While they ate, they discussed the kittens and how ticket sales were going for the fundraiser.

After supper he opened the box containing the cat tree. The assembly was straightforward, but it took longer with two curious kittens trying to help. Olive spent much of the time chasing after screws one of the kittens would bat across the floor.

But he wasn't complaining because that just meant more time spent with Olive and her smile.

He realized as he walked across the street to his place, he didn't experience the usual relief about going home alone after a date. Instead, he was left with a hollow feeling in his chest. As if he was missing out. Missing out on exploring all the mysteries that lurked behind those honey-gold eyes. Missing out on the magic that was Olive.

Chapter Eight

Cal couldn't help glancing across the street to Olive's place before getting into his pickup. It had been almost a week since they'd shared the lasagna and put together the cat tree. They'd met several times for lunch to discuss the upcoming fundraiser, and she'd texted him pictures of kitten hijinks. He glanced across the street again.

Olive's place.

Funny how he'd always thought of it as "the Victorian" until just recently. He had a feeling that from now on, it was going to be Olive's place in his mind, no matter what happened in the future, thanks to the amount of time he was spending there…with her. Although he couldn't imagine her throwing in the towel and giving up on the place. She wasn't a quitter, no matter how soft her heart was.

Of course, she could land herself a husband and start a family to fill up the place. He rubbed his chest. The Mexican food he'd had for lunch must be giving him heartburn. It couldn't be the thought of Olive marrying someone and having children with that guy. It wasn't as if that was what he had planned for his future...even if he'd found himself imagining it once or twice since they'd met.

He opened the driver's door and stopped when he thought he'd heard yelling. Looking across the street, he frowned. The lights were blazing in just about every window on the ground floor.

Was that her running past the window, swinging something that looked like a baseball bat or pole?

Nah. Couldn't be.

Probably nothing. He started to get into the truck but swung back out at the last minute. This was Olive. Better safe than sorry. If this was another spider, he was going to be pissed.

He jogged across the street and took the porch steps two at a time. He went to the door, but it was locked. "Olive?"

Shrieking came from inside.

"No! Please! Don't!"

Damn. Was she in trouble? Loon Lake might be a safe place, but crime wasn't unheard of, even in someplace like this. The residents weren't immune to bad things happening.

He shouted her name again, but she didn't respond directly.

Crash!

"That's it," he yelled. "I'm coming in."

He got a good start and, using his shoulder for leverage, banged against the front door. He bounced off and swore at the ragged pain in his shoulder. Another loud crash. He used all his weight and landed against the door again. The surrounding jamb splintered, and he went flying into the house when the door gave way and swung open. Luckily, he caught himself before ending up in a heap inside the foyer.

Yeah, wouldn't that have been heroic.

He heard another crash coming from the kitchen and he sprinted down the hall.

Inside the kitchen, Olive was swinging a broom. What the...?

"What's going on? I heard the commotion all the way across the street."

"Mayhem happened." She swung again.

"Mayhem? I...oh, you mean the cat." He was still trying to process the situation.

"The door to the cellar was ajar and she went down there."

"So?" he demanded.

"And she came back with *that*," she yelled and pointed.

A mouse was scurrying around in a panic in the corner of the kitchen. It was hemmed in by two kittens, intent on capturing it.

"Do something," Olive implored him.

"You had me or anyone passing by thinking you were in mortal danger," he said, annoyed. But he'd help her, anyway. He scooped up one kitten, then the other. "Do you have somewhere you can stash these two?"

She blinked. "Stash?"

"We don't want them running out after the mouse." Despite the chaos of the situation, he couldn't help noticing his unconscious use of the plural first-person pronoun. When had he started thinking of them as *we*? A unit. The only time he'd been part of one before was when he was with the fire department or as a PJ. Even now as a fire marshal he was somewhat autonomous.

"I have what I used to bring them to the vet." She darted into the laundry room and came back with a cat carrier.

He helped her put the reluctant kittens in the container, swung the metal-grate door shut and set it on the table.

He glanced around the kitchen until he spotted a mop and bucket in the corner. Grabbing the bucket and mop, he turned back to her. "Let's see if we can corral it and I'll dump this over it."

"I don't want to kill it," she said. "I just want it back outside where it belongs."

"I don't want to hurt it, either," he assured her.

In one swift movement, he dumped the bucket over the mouse and held it down.

"My hero," Olive said from behind him.

The rodent scrambled against the edges of the overturned bucket. "It's not over yet," he warned.

"How do we get it outside now?"

"I haven't thought that far ahead," he confessed.

"I guess we could push the bucket toward the back door. Wait, let me clear a path."

He waited while she moved a chair and picked up the scatter rug in front of the sink. Once that was done, he carefully pushed the bucket across the floor to get as close to the door as he could.

"This will be the tricky part."

"I have an idea. Wait right there," she said and ran into the other room.

A minute later she came back with a large dry-erase board. "I'll use this to see that it runs in the right direction and doesn't get back into the house."

"Good thinking," he said and opened the door to the backyard. "Ready?"

"As I'll ever be."

He carefully lifted one end of the bucket and shoved it toward the open door. Evidently the mouse was smart, and it ran toward freedom and disappeared into the backyard.

"Thank you. Again."

He frowned. She might be thanking him, but she sounded anything but grateful. Normally, he didn't go looking for trouble when it came to women, but he couldn't let this drop. "What's wrong?"

He set down the bucket by the door.

"It's not that I'm not grateful but I am a capable adult."

"Have I ever implied you weren't?" If he couldn't understand his actions, how was he supposed to give her an explanation?

"You keep rushing over here," she said, lifting her chin.

"Then that's my problem, not yours."

She opened her mouth, furrowed her brow and closed her mouth again without speaking.

The kittens started protesting and she opened the carrier.

He crossed to the cellar door and shut it. When she met his gaze, he shrugged. "They obviously don't share your reluctance about going into the basement."

"Hey! I…" Her shoulders slumped. "If that mouse was an example of what's down there, I stand by my reluctance."

"I can get you the name of an—"

"Exterminator," she said, finishing for him. "Is there anyone you don't know?"

"What can I say? I grew up in Loon Lake. A lot of the people I went to school with are now working at or running businesses." He watched the struggle playing out on her face. Yup. Too tenderhearted for her own good. "I'm sure they can trap and relocate any unwanted visitors, if that's what's bothering you."

"Do you think so?"

"Just smile and I'm sure they'll make an exception in your case." What the hell made him say that? He wasn't even sure why her attitude toward life bothered him so much.

She scowled. "What's that supposed to mean?"

Yeah, Pope, what does it mean?

"I just…" He hung his head and studied the tops of his boots. "I'm sorry. I shouldn't have said that."

She hissed out her breath and sent the kittens scrambling under the kitchen table. "Is that what you think? That I would try to—to flirt or whatever it was you were implying to get people to do things for me?"

"No! Of course not. You're not like that." The effect her smile had on him was all about him. Not her. But he wasn't about to admit that.

"Is that what people think?"

"No." He put a hand on her shoulder. "Your smile is infectious."

She scrunched up her nose. "Like a disease?"

"No, like laughter is contagious." Oh, God. He had no business getting into this type of conversation.

She sputtered a laugh and he said, "On that note, I'll be leaving."

* * *

She was behind him on the way down the hall. Her gasp when they reached the front entryway made him wince.

"What did you do to my front door?"

"Oh, yeah…about that…" How could that have slipped his mind? "It was locked, and I had to get in."

"So you went all Neanderthal fireman on it?"

"No. I left my ax in my other pants, so there was nothing fireman about it." He rubbed his shoulder. Now that the excitement was winding down, it was beginning to throb.

Her eyes widened. "You mean you broke in using brute strength?"

"Just like in the movies." He nodded. Yeah, his actions had been stupid, but he seemed to act that way when it came to her.

Her demeanor changed from irritated to concerned and she rushed over to him. "Let me see. Did you hurt your shoulder? What were you thinking? You could have dislocated it or broken it or something."

"What was I thinking? Let's see… With you yelling threats and banging around… I didn't stop to think. I just knew I needed to get to you. Fast." The explanation had come spilling out of him. What was he doing by practically admitting how much she'd come to mean to him?

"I'm sorry. I didn't even hear you."

"Is there anything more you're frightened of? Something I should be aware of? How do you feel about snakes?" He was trying to backpedal by acting glib, but the truth was, he was embarrassed and in pain from his shoulder.

She took hold of his arm and marched him back into the kitchen. He was too shocked—and yeah, maybe a little turned on—by her behavior to protest.

"Sit," she said as she hooked her foot around a kitchen chair and pulled it out. "Let me get something for that shoulder bruise."

He sat and watched her go to the refrigerator, open the freezer and pull out a bag of frozen vegetables.

Slapping the bag against his shoulder, she said, "I know it's cliché but so is your method of— Oh, my God. My door."

She scurried from the room. He swore and followed her from the room but held the frozen bag against the throb in his shoulder.

She stood with her hands on her hips and surveyed the damage done.

He refused to feel bad about the door. He'd thought she was in danger. So sue him. He was going to set her straight and— She turned around and the look of distress on her face had him dropping the peas and carrots onto a table in the foyer.

"I'll get it repaired," he promised. What? So much for all that tough talk from less than a minute ago. What was it about this woman that had him wishing things could be different? That *he* could be different. The kind of guy who could say forever and mean it. But that wasn't him, and he needed to remember that.

"But—but what about tonight? What am I supposed to do?"

"You could always come and stay at my place." He'd meant it as a joke. Or had he? He might not believe in forever but there was always today. Or tonight.

"I can't leave the kittens."

"They're welcome, too." You can bring anyone you want if it means— *No! Don't go down that path.*

You're always trying to protect her. Do it now and protect her from yourself.

"But what if someone does come along? They wouldn't even have to break in to clean me out."

He glanced around at the sparsely furnished foyer and adjoining front parlor.

"Not another word," she warned.

"I didn't even say anything." He started to lift his shoulder but winced and dropped it.

She grimaced, then picked up the vegetables and handed the bag to him. "This won't help if you don't use it."

He held the bag to his shoulder. Damn but that would teach him to try and be a hero. "I've got some wood in my garage. I can do something temporary for tonight. You won't be able to use the door until it's properly fixed, but no one will get in."

"Thanks." *And there goes the possibility of Olive staying the night*, he mused with an internal sigh. A good thing, even if it didn't feel like it.

While Cal went to get the supplies to fix her door, she went to get the baby playpen she'd bought at a consignment shop. The mesh-sided structure was good for corralling the kittens. She preferred putting them in there, rather than locking them up in the bathroom or laundry room. Of course, it wouldn't take long before they'd be escaping, but she hoped by then they'd be bigger and not as likely to come to harm. Tonight, she just didn't want them to be trying to get out the open front door or bother Cal while he worked.

Although she couldn't imagine him getting upset over them getting in his way. Just like with his friends' kids, he seemed very tolerant.

And she was spending way too much time thinking about her sexy neighbor.

Contrary to what she'd overheard him say about her on the hunt for a husband, she wasn't actively seeking a spouse. But if she let herself get hung up on someone who wasn't suitable, how could she be open to someone else?

She set up the playpen and heard plastic crinkling.

Going to the other side of the couch, she caught Mischief attacking the bag of frozen vegetables.

"How did you get that?" she asked.

She reached for the bag, but kitten claws had dug in and it ripped, spilling peas and carrots all over the floor.

"Great. See what you've done," she scolded, but didn't put any rancor into her tone.

The kitten sisters were now batting errant peas around the hardwood floor.

"Need some help?"

She pressed a hand to her chest. "You startled me."

"Sorry," he said, his lips twitching. "At least I wasn't a spider or a mouse."

"Careful. I still have my broom."

He opened his mouth as if he wanted to say something but closed it again and shook his head. "Nope. Not gonna go there."

"Smart choice," she said and laughed. Even if he had said what was probably on his mind, she wouldn't have taken offense. Now that she knew him a little better, she enjoyed the sparring they sometimes engaged in.

Sure, he could be a bit zealous when it came to his job, but she understood now that it was because he cared, not because he enjoyed a power trip.

"Umm, Olive?"

"What?"

"I think you will need that broom." He pointed to the mess on the floor.

She laughed. "I'll go get it, but first these little monsters go in the playpen."

"That's a clever idea," he said.

"Thanks. I'm not just another pretty face," she joked.

"That's for sure."

She looked up. "Oh, I didn't mean…"

He laid a hand on her arm, and his touch seemed to flood her entire body with warmth. "I know you didn't, but take it from me, I think you're pretty special."

She blinked and swallowed. If she didn't move away, she was going to throw herself into his arms. "Well, um, I…uh, I should go get that broom."

"I'll put these rascals into confinement."

In the kitchen she stood for a moment, her hands braced on the sink. She needed to remember that if she gave in to her desire for Cal, her actions could ruin not only their friendship, but it would also have a domino effect. She loved her new life. She loved Loon Lake and her special home, even if it needed numerous and probably expensive repairs. But, best of all, she loved the group of friends she'd found here. They had become like a family to her.

As much as she wanted it, she wasn't going to jeopardize any of that with a fling.

Chapter Nine

Cal scooped up his keys from the counter in his kitchen and let himself out the side door to the driveway. He'd decided to take up Brody on his offer to see the inner workings of Camp Life Launch and the plans the Wilsons had for expansion. As cochair of the committee raising funds for the new bunkhouse, he felt it was his duty to learn as much as he could.

This wouldn't be the same as going there to pass out ice cream and kick a soccer ball around.

Outside, he stopped to stare over at Olive's place. It had been three days since the mouse incident. He'd gone the next night and repaired her door. He still needed to add a coat or two of polyurethane on the new wood, but he'd been dragging his feet. Not because he didn't want to see Olive, but because he did. And that was the problem. He wanted to see her a little too much.

"You're acting like a lovesick schoolboy," he scolded himself as he pressed the key fob and unlocked his Tacoma.

"Mooning over the girl next door," he muttered as he slammed his door.

He pulled out of his driveway with one last glance at the Victorian. He still hadn't repaired her porch swing and— No! A little space, a couple more days and he'd get this—this…whatever he was feeling for Olive under control. Then he'd go and help with some of her repairs, including staining and weatherproofing around her front door.

Driving through town, he waved at a few people who recognized him and his pickup. He probably could have gone anywhere after he'd left the air force but there was something about Loon Lake, with its friendly people and quintessential New England architecture, that called to him. That's why he could understand Olive's love of the town and her determination to succeed here. He'd do this without giving in to his physical desires.

He didn't want to see disappointment in her eyes when he failed to be the man she wanted and deserved.

Outside of town he followed the state highway until he reached the county road that led to Camp

Life Launch. The road climbed one of the rolling hills Vermont was famous for, past pastures and dense stands of sugar maples. Those trees would be tapped in February and March and the collected sap boiled down into the different grades of maple syrup. Not only did the trees provide the sweet syrup, but they also put on a show in the fall, when their leaves turned vibrant shades of yellow, burnt orange and red.

Yeah, he'd dreamed of being back home while serving in Afghanistan.

He turned off the county road and a white two-story farmhouse with a gleaming red metal roof came into view. The farm sat on a large tract of flat land. A covered porch ran across the front and wrapped around one side of the home, similar to Olive's veranda, but this house had simple clean lines, as did the covered porch. And off to one side stood a large red barn with white-painted split-rail fencing. Next to the barn stood a restored bunkhouse. Cal had been a rookie on the Loon Lake Fire Department when the bunkhouse had caught fire and been partially burned.

It was soon after the fire that Brody and Mary had gotten together and married. They now had two children, although Cal knew Brody had adopted Elliott, Mary's infant son from a previous relationship. You only had to see the couple together to know how happy they were.

Okay, so healthy relationships did exist. An image

of long, blond curls and a smile that lit up the world slipped into his mind. He shook his head to try and dispel it and concentrated on his driving.

Cal pulled his truck into a gravel parking area between the barn and bunkhouse. He parked and got out. Mary had an office in part of the building where the fire had been.

Watery clucking and a loud scuffle caught his attention. Beyond the bunkhouse and closer to the home was a weathered wooden coop with fluffy chickens crisscrossing the enclosed space surrounding it. The noisy scuffle was between two brownish hens, who were trying to establish a pecking order.

"Got any ice cream this time, Mr. Cal?" asked a small voice.

He turned away from the birds toward the voice. A towheaded boy ran toward him from the side of the barn.

"Sorry. No ice cream this time." Cal held up his hands as if to back up his comment.

"That's okay." The boy looked disappointed but shrugged, as if he were used to disappointment.

Cal's stomach tensed as he thought of Olive. How often had she felt that way after entering foster care?

"Mr. Brody said you flew in helicopters and sometimes even jumped from them. Is that true?"

Cal nodded and the boy's eyes widened. He searched his memory. "You're Andrew, right?"

The boy's head bobbed up and down.

Three more adolescent boys came around the barn and headed toward them.

Andrew looked over his shoulder. "Mr. Cal's gonna tell us all about what it was like flying in a helicopter."

"I am?" Cal said, but his words were drowned out by the chorus of "Cool" and "Awesome" from the other boys.

Cal looked at their eager faces. Looked like war stories were just as welcome as ice cream for these boys. He'd have to sanitize the language and leave out some of the details, but he could tell them a few stories. He wouldn't glorify war, nor would he give them stark reality, so he searched for something in between. He knew enough about young boys to know they liked a certain amount of gore in their stories.

"Did you ever get scared?" one asked after he'd related a few stories.

"All the time." Huh. He hadn't given that a lot of thought because he was still able to do his job. So why couldn't he set aside his fears regarding a relationship with Olive? He might not have known her all that long, but he believed she was trustworthy.

"Look!" Andrew pointed to one of the fenced pastures. "The horses are out. Maybe we can ride now."

The boys started to race off but turned back to shout "thanks."

"Upstaged by horses," Cal said, shaking his head.

"Andrew loves 'em and those other boys follow his lead."

Cal half turned to find a boy of about thirteen had hung back. "And you don't follow Andrew's lead?"

"Nah. I'd rather find out what you did when you got scared."

"You're sure you wouldn't rather go horseback riding?" Cal asked, half joking. The boy continued to stare at him. Cal sighed. "Tell me your name and I'll tell you some of the ways we had for dealing with fear."

"I'm David Wells."

"Nice to meet you, David." Cal stuck his hand out. The boy looked surprised but shook hands. "One way of dealing with the fear was to laugh about it. This world can be a crazy place and learning to laugh about scary or bad things helps."

He thought for a moment, then nodded. "Is it like the cop shows I watch? Why they make jokes?"

"I guess it is." Cal leaned closer and made a point of lowering his voice. "But be careful making jokes. Some it might be best to keep in your head and just use against the fear."

"You mean because I'm still a kid?"

And a smart one at that. Cal nodded. "Breathing also helps."

David gave him a skeptical look. "Breathing?"

"Next time your heart is pounding, or your knees

feel like jelly, take a breath, hold it in for four seconds, then slowly let it out for four seconds."

Cal demonstrated and David grinned. "That's pretty cool. Thanks."

Cal noticed David kept glancing over to where two alpacas had come to the split-rail fence by the barn. "More friends of yours?"

David blushed and shrugged. "I save the raisins from my snack for them."

"Do you have some now?" Cal asked. David nodded and Cal continued, "Got enough to share so we can both feed them?"

"Sure," David said and looked relieved.

They ambled over to the fence and David dug into his pocket. He pulled out a small box of raisins and shook some into Cal's outstretched palm. David let the alpaca nibble the raisins from his hand. "You're a friend of Miss Olive's, aren't you?"

Had Olive mentioned him to this boy? "Yeah, she and I are neighbors…" Could he classify Olive as a friend?

"She said you were," David said, a note of suspicion in his tone.

"And she's right. We started as neighbors but now we're friends. Are you and she friends, too?"

"Yeah, we talk when she comes here."

Cal was getting the sense David wanted to say more. "What do you talk about?"

The boy hesitated and Cal rushed on, "Sorry. It's

probably none of my business. You don't have to tell me."

David shook out some more raisins for the waiting alpacas. "She told me how she was in foster care, too."

Cal felt the boy's gaze on him. "Yeah, she told me, too."

The kid let out his breath. Had he been worried he'd broken a confidence? "It's not a secret," Cal said, hoping to reassure him.

"I asked her about getting adopted and Miss Olive told me that the chances of getting adopted after the age of eleven are slim."

Why in the world would Olive say something cruel like that to this boy? That didn't sound like the warm, compassionate woman he knew.

Before Cal could think of something to say that might make the kid feel better, David said hurriedly, "She told me she never got a permanent placement, either. I guess if someone as nice as Miss Olive didn't get adopted, then it's not our fault. People just like babies, I guess. She told me about something she called statistics."

"Statistics?"

"Yeah, she said that all those numbers weren't because of anything I did or didn't do. It's just the way things are sometimes." The kid blushed. "She told me it wasn't because I have to wear glasses or that I have crooked teeth. At first I thought she was just saying stuff to make me feel better, ya know?"

Cal nodded, still unsure what value anything he said would have. But he did make a mental note to ask if he could help the kid afford braces if he needed them. No matter his living situation. He'd probably have to ask Olive or the Wilsons how any of that worked. *I thought I wasn't supposed to care about any kid like I was their dad?* he thought ruefully, adding, *I just want some kids to have what I didn't. If I can do something good, why not?*

"I mean," David continued, "Miss Olive is so pretty she would've gotten adopted right away if it weren't for those statistics things."

Cal opened his mouth to explain the meaning behind statistics but closed it again without saying a word. Olive's words had made the boy feel better, so who was he to bring the kid down?

"Ya know what I mean, Mr. Cal?"

"Yes, I do."

If Cal had needed proof that fatherhood wasn't for him, this was it. It was one to kick a soccer ball around with Elliott or shoot hoops with some of the older boys at the camp, but being responsible for a developing human's well-being was a whole different story. How could he be sure he wouldn't mess up the kid, like his own dad had with him?

How could he trust that he'd pick the right woman? His mom probably thought she'd picked the right man to spend her life with, have a child with. And she hadn't. He wouldn't be any woman's mistake.

But Olive would never turn her back, a voice inside his head scolded. She couldn't even turn her back on half-dead plants, for heaven's sake. She'd spent time nursing them back to life. The same way she was nursing the kittens, turning them from skinny, mangy, flea-bitten creatures to healthy, energetic balls of fluff.

"Isn't that right, Mr. Cal?"

"What?" Cal glanced at David, who was looking up at him, and he felt an immediate pang of guilt for not paying attention to the boy. He'd been so deep in thought—about his lovely neighbor—that he'd almost forgotten about this child. Shame on him. It would be easy to blame Olive for distracting him, but that wouldn't be fair, and he liked to think he was, if not much else, fair.

But had he been fair? He'd been blaming his parents for his attitude toward marriage and commitment, but he was an adult now. Past the point where he could blame his current attitudes on his childhood. When did he stop letting the past cripple him and take responsibility for his actions?

The past might never be forgotten but it could be forgiven. And that's the part he needed to work on.

What happened to him had molded and shaped him, but it wasn't all bad. He'd overcome a lot to become a PJ. Training took not just physical agility but mental stamina as well. Did that last component come from what he'd endured when his life fell apart? Maybe that explained why he'd completed training when at least 80 percent of candidates drop out.

Shaking his head to clear it, he turned to the boy. "I'm sorry, David, could you repeat that?"

Olive pulled in to a spot in the gravel parking lot at Camp Life Launch. She'd spoken with Mary about the intricacies of running your own business. Mary had suggested Olive come and see for herself some of the systems she'd put into place. Of course, Mary was an accountant, so she had the advantage of putting her background to work. But it wouldn't hurt to absorb some of the other woman's expertise. Olive had her own strengths in event planning, and they might be able to combine their knowledge and help one another.

She got out of the car and headed toward the bunkhouse that also housed Mary's office. The door opened and Cal stepped out.

Olive stumbled a step at seeing him but recovered. She glanced over at the other vehicles parked by the barn. Why hadn't she noticed his pickup? "What are you doing here?" She pulled her lips in, regretting her tone as much as her question. His whereabouts was none of her business, but his presence had her senses on high alert.

"I could ask you the same thing?"

"I'm sorry for sounding so rude," she said, feeling the heat blazing in her cheeks. "It's just that I'm surprised to run into you here."

He raised his eyebrows. "And why is that?"

She opened her mouth, but no words came out. "I didn't realize you volunteered with the kids."

"To be honest, I came out here to familiarize myself with the business end of things since we're raising money for the place."

"Checking that they're following the fire codes?" she asked, her tongue pressed firmly against her cheek.

He pressed a hand against his chest. "You wound me, Olive."

"As if that were possible." She sucked in air, unsure if he was joking. "I'm sorry... I—I never..."

"Speak like that?" He reached out and brushed a stray curl off her cheek. "Maybe you should. I don't want to see you get hurt."

The combination of his tender touch and his words had her confused, unnerved. Who was he warning her away from? She swallowed. "Who would want to hurt me?"

"It's not a question of want, Olive." He sighed. "You—you're..."

"I'm what?" If he called her naive, she might just slap him upside the head.

"It's not you, it's—"

"You're not going to give me an it's-not-you, it's-me speech, are you?"

"Of course not."

He might be denying it, but she detected guilt in his face and tone. She must have given him a skeptical look because he rushed on. "I'm just saying that guys aren't always honest about what they want."

"But not you, right? Because you've already told me how you're not interested in settling down or starting a family. So, you're off the hook."

Awkward much, Olive? She should've kept her mouth shut. Things hadn't changed much since adolescence after all.

He looked as though he was trying to figure out how to respond. "Well, I am what I'd call settled since I'm gainfully employed and own my own home. And you're right about me not wanting to start my own family. That doesn't mean I don't like kids or aren't interested in doing what little I can to help them or the Wilsons' efforts."

She regretted her insensitive comments, but she couldn't undo what had already been said. So she continued to go for a straightforward approach. "I'm sorry. You're right. I had no business saying those things."

"Well, this is a change," he said, his tone far from upset.

Could she salvage this? "What do you mean?"

"Usually, I'm the one needing to apologize to you."

"Oh, that. If you're referring to what I overheard at the McBride cookout, I told you I forgave you for what you said. If I hadn't been eavesdropping, I would have been none the wiser."

"I still shouldn't have said it, and you may have forgiven me but that doesn't mean I've forgiven myself."

She touched him, laying her fingers over the warmth of his forearm, and did her best to ignore the jolt of pleasure she got from the skin-to-skin contact. "Please tell me you're not fretting over that. It's over and done with."

"You're so gracious it makes me want to confess my sins." He took her hand in his, cradling it, and shook his head. "That day I came out here with Tavie's ice cream, I did it because it seemed the most expedient thing to do. It got Tavie off my back about her ice cream melting and I got points for doing a good deed. And today, I was using the excuse that I should learn more about the business end of things. But I really did enjoy interacting with the kids and wanted to come back."

"These kids draw you in, don't they?"

"You could say that."

"I am saying that," she responded lightly, but pulled her hand from his. As much as she enjoyed the contact—and boy, was she enjoying it—she needed to step back. He scrambled her wits and touching him made it worse.

Cal wanted to grab her hand back, even started to reach out, but let his hand drop to his side. "David told me how you made him feel better."

"He did?"

She seemed surprised. Why? Surely, her own experience meant that she must realize she knew what to say to these kids, and he said so.

She shook her head. "Every time I leave here, I get a painful lump in my stomach worried that I said the wrong thing to one of these children. That I somehow made a situation worse instead of better."

He was shocked by her comment. "I thought I was the only one who felt that way about maybe messing up a young life."

"About me, you mean?"

"No, silly—" he touched the end of her nose, let his finger trail across her cheek "—about me. I had no idea what to say to David."

"Neither did I, except to tell him the truth. If I had started blowing happily-ever-after smoke, he would have me pegged for a fraud, so I did the best I could with the truth. Or at least, the truth according to Olive Downing."

"I thought you believed in happily-ever-after. So why would talking about that type of thing be like blowing smoke? Are you telling me you don't believe in it? That you've been putting on a front all this time?" His chest constricted. He hated that he was giving her a hard time, but couldn't seem to stop himself. She rubbed up against some part buried deep, causing that fight-or-flight response.

She pulled away again and scowled at him. "Doesn't that cynicism you lug around ever get heavy?"

"I'm a realist," he admitted. He was glad she'd stepped away, put some breathing room between them. Yup, very glad.

"How can you look at your friends and not believe in it? Brody and Mary live it every day. As do Ellie and Liam, and Meg and Riley. Just because I didn't come from a happy beginning doesn't mean I can't have a happy ending."

"Then what's your point? Either you believe or you don't." Why was he continuing to argue with her? It wasn't as if he was going to let her convince him. Was he?

"The fact I believe in it doesn't mean it's guaranteed for everyone. As I tried to convey to David, you have to play with the hand you're dealt. Did I tell you he's been teaching me poker?"

He grabbed at the change of subject. "Is he any good?"

"Better than me. Do you play?"

Her smile made his heart do that stumbling thing and it took a few extra seconds for her words to reach his ears, for his brain to process them. "As a matter of fact, I do. Some of the guys at the firehouse get together with a couple of the EMTs for a poker night. Care to join us?"

"David warned me I needed to develop my poker face before I was ready for the big time."

"You and Colton, one of the EMTs we play with, should get together. He's been practicing his poker face since he figured out we knew his tells."

"Maybe I'll give him a call."

He laughed because he knew she was joking, but his gut tightened all the same. Colton was single, not safely married like the rest of the guys he played with.

You can't have it both ways.

And he hadn't changed his mind about what he wanted for his future. But the more time he spent with Olive, the less certain he became about his choices. A future without her sounded less and less appealing.

Chapter Ten

Juggling a six-pack in one hand and pizza in the other, Cal closed the passenger door with his hip. It had been a week since he'd run into Olive at the camp. They'd planned to get together to discuss the fundraiser, but he'd had to spend several days out of town to testify on an arson case he'd been consulted on and had just gotten back.

He hated to admit how much he missed seeing her and those rascally kittens. He bet she wasn't having takeout tonight. His stomach rumbled at the thought of her chicken and dumplings, or chicken cacciatore. Sitting in her kitchen and eating a home-cooked meal had been weirdly comforting. He glanced at the pizza box. Maybe he could... He pushed aside that thought.

It wasn't as if he needed comforting. So what if his bachelor life suddenly didn't seem as satisfying as it once had been? He'd had ups and downs before. Not just in life but in his career, too. Of course, when that failed to satisfy him the way it used to, he'd left the air force. But he knew why that had gone sideways for him and he'd taken action.

As comforting and alluring as he found Olive, forever wasn't in the cards for him. He didn't need anyone depending on him, just as he didn't want to depend on anyone. He didn't want anyone having the power to hurt him. Been there. Done that.

That thought made him think of his comments at the cookout. Once again, he regretted those words. And his regret stemmed from the hurtful declaration and not the fact he'd gotten caught. Liam had been right; Olive was a genuinely nice person and didn't deserve him putting her down.

He glanced across the street and frowned. There she was in her driveway heading toward her car, but something seemed off about her movements. Moving slowly, she held her arm close to her chest.

"Olive?" he called, taking a few steps toward the end of his driveway. "Something wrong?"

"Huh? Oh, I fell. I think I may have done something to my wrist." She grimaced as she tried to lift her arm.

"Let me take a look." He stepped closer to the end of his driveway.

"I don't want to interrupt your supper," she said, hitching her chin at the stuff in his hands.

He glanced down at the pizza and beer. Huh. He'd forgotten he was still carrying it. He turned back, set both in the bed of his truck and sprinted across the street.

"Let me take a look." He realized she was an adult and perfectly capable of looking after herself. So why was he always so quick to jump in? Not because she needed it, but because *he* did. Well, he didn't need it but he definitely wanted it. He liked helping her.

"That isn't necessary. I'm sure I—"

"Don't argue with me," he said as his training kicked in. "Let me make an assessment and then decide what is necessary in this situation."

She blinked at him and opened her mouth, but no sound came out. Good. He didn't want to argue with her, but he was in charge.

"Damn, what did you do to yourself?" he asked. His tone was rough, but he made sure his touch was gentle as he lifted her hand. Her wrist had swelled to about the size of grapefruit and was beginning to get colorful. "Can you wiggle your fingers?"

She winced but managed to move the fingers.

"It could be a distal radius fracture. Are the fingers numb?"

She nodded and sucked in a breath.

"Okay. Let's get some ice on it to help with the swelling and then get you to the ER for X-rays."

"I was on my way to the hospital," she insisted.

"You were driving yourself?"

"No, I called an Uber."

"Try again, Olive. This is Loon Lake. There are no Uber drivers." He admired her determination, but her actions still angered him. *Because you worry about her*, a little voice said. He pushed it away and glared at her. "You should have called me."

"You weren't home when I did it."

"But I'm here now. I'll get what we need and drive you to the hospital." He was already going over protocol in his head for a broken wrist. It might not be broken but he wasn't taking any chances. Not with Olive.

"I'm capable of driving myself."

"We're wasting time." He cupped his hand under her elbow and guided her toward the end of the driveway. "C'mon, you're not driving yourself to the hospital."

"Well, I'm not calling an ambulance."

Why was she arguing with him? He considered telling her he knew best but took one look at the stubborn set of her chin and decided against it. "Humor me by letting me take you to the hospital."

"But—"

"No *buts*. Helping people is what I was trained to do and I'm doing it. No arguments."

Once he got her across the street, he led her into

his kitchen and used his foot to pull out a chair and sat her down.

"But…" she sputtered. "I thought you were taking me to the hospital."

"I am, but first we're going to ice it." He let go of her and opened the freezer portion of his refrigerator.

"Wouldn't it be better to just go to the ER?" she asked.

"In a perfect world, but if we have to wait for treatment, this will slow the swelling and help make you more comfortable while we do." He made an ice pack and grabbed a few towels hanging over the handle on the oven door.

He helped her wrap the towel and put the ice pack against the swelling. He then took the other towel and formed it into a sling to immobilize the arm and lift it over her heart. He tied the towel at the top of her shoulder to secure it.

"Is all this necessary?"

"It will help," he snapped. She jerked her head back and he mumbled, "Sorry."

"No, I'm sorry for arguing."

He stared at her for a moment before admitting, "Tempers rise when you care."

"Thank you," she said, her lips trembling.

He ground his teeth at the whole situation. In the past he'd always been able to remain objective about a patient, even fellow soldiers, but not so with Olive.

What happened to all his emotional detachment? *That's long since gone out the window.*

Once at the hospital, he pulled the truck into the parking lot. "Do you want me to drop you off in front of the entrance?"

"That's okay. I can walk from the car."

"If you're sure."

She nodded and he pulled into a parking spot as close to the emergency entrance as he could. Scrambling out, he jogged to the other side of the pickup. She'd gotten the door open and had swung her feet over the side. He didn't want her jarring her arm by jumping out of the truck.

"Let me," he said and grabbed her around the waist and lifted her out. He gently set her on the ground. "Want me to go and hunt down a wheelchair?"

"A wheelchair? It's my wrist, not my legs."

"Of course, I could always carry you."

"What? No! I…" She glanced up at him. She clicked her tongue against her front teeth, but her eyes were soft, free from censure. "You're messing with me."

"Sort of." He took her uninjured arm and began to gently guide her to the entrance. "But I am willing to carry you, if need be."

Her response was a small laugh he found reassuring, which was weird but now wasn't the time to explore his feelings for Olive.

At the entrance, he guided her through a pair of glass doors that whooshed open. Entering a small waiting area, they spied a nurse seated at a desk.

"Hi, I'm Stacy." The woman smiled as she greeted them, but her assessing gaze zeroed in on Olive's wrist. "Oh, dear, looks like you've done a number on that poor wrist. Let's get your intake done so we can get you patched up, although it looks as though someone has already seen to your comfort."

Cal felt heat rise to his cheeks as he guided Olive to the seat in front of the desk and didn't let go of her arm until she was safely in the chair. He settled into the seat beside her.

"It was part of his previous job," Olive explained. *Yeah, that's it*, he thought sarcastically.

"Oh. Were you an EMT?" The nurse gave him an appreciative gaze.

"Sort of." He shrugged. What did any of that matter? Olive was what mattered here. "She's obviously in a lot of pain so if she could be seen by a doctor. "

"Well, of course. But we do need to gather some information first."

"Can't that wait?" His knee started bouncing up and down as if it had a mind of its own. What was wrong with him? He knew Olive was in no danger and that this was simply hospital procedure. But, damn it, this was *Olive* and he wanted her examined and treated as soon as possible.

Olive put her good hand on his knee, gently pressing down to stop it from jiggling. "It's okay," she told him. "The ice is helping. Everything you did is helping. Remember, you said that's why you were stopping to do that before we came?"

He blew his breath out noisily through his lips. Why was she the one comforting him? "You're right."

"The sooner we get the information, the sooner she can be seen by our physician."

The nurse began asking Olive questions and he tried to remain patient while she answered them.

Olive paused and, clearing her throat, gave him a pointed look. He glanced down at his bouncing knee and grinned.

"Sorry," he muttered.

Another nurse came in with a wheelchair and introduced herself as Jan. She indicated Cal's ministrations and said, "Somebody knew what they were doing."

"That's what I said," Stacy said as Jan began to wheel her away.

Cal insisted on accompanying Olive into the examination room. *He's been with me every step of the way*, she marveled.

"We'll need to get an X-ray," Jan said as she wheeled her into a room. Her gaze bounced between the two of them. "Is there any chance you could be pregnant?"

"Absolutely not." Olive could feel herself blush and didn't dare make eye contact with Cal.

He cleared his throat but didn't make any other response. Too bad she couldn't see what he was thinking. Or maybe it was good that she couldn't.

Because he's probably wishing he'd let me drive myself, she thought.

He acted like he wanted to accompany her to get her wrist x-rayed, but Jan pointed to a chair in the room and told him to stay put.

"I'll have Olive back to you in a jiff," Jan said as she wheeled her out.

Despite the pain in her wrist, Olive reacted to Jan's phrasing. *Back to you.* As if she belonged with him. If only…

While wheeling her to get the wrist scanned, the nurse chatted about buying a ticket for the fundraiser, and Olive wished her luck.

"Talk about luck. You're the luckiest one of all. Winning Sadie's place. I've always loved that place."

"So do I," Olive told her and sucked in a breath as the nurse undid the things Cal had put in place. She helped her out of the chair, put the shields on her and got her arm in position.

"And the neighbors aren't bad, either. Hmm?" Jan said.

"Oh, no, we're not… We…we're just…" She trailed off. What were they? Surely more than neighbors. "Friends," she finally said. They were at least that much.

Jan patted her shoulder. "Let me just get some pictures of this."

After getting what she needed, Jan wheeled her back to the room. And Cal.

Before Jan could help her back onto the gurney, Cal stepped forward and assisted.

"The doctor should be in shortly."

After the nurse left, Cal began to pace.

"You can leave if you'd like," she told him.

He stopped his movements and glared at her. "I brought you. I'll bring you home."

"But I don't know how long this could—"

He put a finger over her lips. "It will take as long as it takes."

He dropped his hand, and she placed her uninjured one on his arm. "Thank you. This has been easier with you here."

He shrugged. "It's always easier going through something like this with someone."

"No. I meant having *you* with me. I—"

Before she could finish, the doctor entered and introduced himself. "I'm Dr. Crimmins. I've had a look at the X-rays, and you have a distal radius fracture. In other words, you've broken your wrist.

"How did this happen?" Dr. Crimmins asked as he manipulated her fingers.

Olive blushed and glanced over to Cal, who was

leaning against the wall. "I tripped coming down the stairs and used my hand to try and catch myself. It's all my own fault."

"I see." The physician gave Cal a pointed glance before pushing his glasses up his nose. He spent a few moments making a note on her chart.

The doctor's attitude finally sank in, and Olive knew she would have to confess. She couldn't have anyone thinking Cal might be responsible. Even in small towns, domestic abuse occurred, and she imagined ER personnel would be naturally suspicious. In a roundabout way Cal was, since he'd brought the kittens to her, but she certainly didn't blame him for the kittens' behavior. "It was Mayhem."

"Mayhem?" The doctor furrowed his brow. "I don't—"

Cal straightened up and stepped away from the wall. "You mean to tell me one of those kittens is responsible for this?"

Not wanting the doctor to be thinking poorly of Cal for even one second longer, she addressed him first. "Mayhem is my kitten."

She turned to Cal. "No. I'm responsible. She was just being a kitten." She knew Cal would never harm the kitten, but she also didn't want him blaming Mayhem, either. "It was just a freak accident. I could just as easily have tripped over something else."

"Luckily, it's a clean break so a cast is all that's needed while the bone mends," said Dr. Crimmins, who seemed reassured that this really was an accident. "We'll fix you up with a fiberglass cast. Those are lighter and more breathable."

"How long will I have to wear it?"

"Four to six weeks."

Olive groaned and Cal rested a hand on her shoulder. "At least there's no surgery involved."

"True." The doctor nodded and stuck his pen in his pocket. "I'll leave a prescription order for pain pills. You may need some tonight to sleep. I'll have the nurse fill out the paperwork and give you a list of orthopedic doctors for a follow-up appointment for cast removal and if you have any problems."

He turned to Cal. "I heard you did a good job with reducing swelling and keeping the wrist immobilized before bringing her in. Since the swelling isn't bad, we'll put the cast on now."

"Smells like markers," she said and wrinkled her nose as the doctor put the layers on.

Standing beside her, Cal huffed out a breath. "Does it feel warm, too?"

She nodded and glanced up at him. "You've had a broken bone?"

"Once as a kid and once as an adult. My left arm and my right wrist on separate occasions." He chuckled. "Both times playing sports."

Olive rolled her eyes. "Much more manly than tripping over a cat. Hmm?"

"That's my story and I'm sticking to it," he said and winked.

The doctor laughed and gave verbal instructions on keeping it clean and dry. "And no sticking an object in there to scratch it."

The doctor left and Jan the nurse brought in the paperwork for her to sign. "Lucky you're left-handed," she commented as Olive signed the papers.

"Yeah, leaving smudge marks on all my school papers is finally paying off."

She threw Cal a puzzled frown when she saw his fierce scowl. "Is my being left-handed going to be a problem?"

He shook his head. "Not at all. I—I had no idea."

"That's okay. I forgive you. Besides, I'm ambidextrous. I write strictly left-handed but use my right for a majority of other things."

He grunted and went to get his pickup.

As Jan wheeled her out, she couldn't help wondering why Cal had seemed almost distraught. Maybe it was some sort of delayed reaction. "Maybe he just doesn't like left-handers," she muttered under her breath.

"Oh, he likes you just fine." Olive glanced up and Jan continued, "I've seen the way he looks at you."

Cal jumped into the truck and started it. The fact Olive was left-handed didn't matter. What mattered was that he wanted to learn everything that made her tick. He wanted to know her inside and out. That fact should have had him running. And yet he was upset because she hadn't turned to him. She'd been injured and she hadn't called him.

She had turned to him when she needed help with an electrical fuse. So why hadn't she called him today? This was a lot more serious than a blown fuse. Didn't she think he could be counted on?

For the first time in a long, long time, he wanted to be that guy and she obviously hadn't felt like that.

He pulled up to the entrance to the ER and got out of the truck.

Jan put a supporting arm around Olive as she started to get up.

Cal rushed over. "I got her."

Jan dropped her arm. "Of course."

He wanted to say something to the nurse, but that would be denying his feelings and he couldn't bring himself to do that. Instead, he nodded and helped Olive into the passenger seat. Once she was settled, he reached over her to fasten her seat belt.

"Take care of her," Jan called as she turned back toward the entrance, and Cal gave her a salute.

He got back into the driver's seat but didn't immediately start the engine.

Olive shifted in her seat. "Something wrong?"

He glanced over at her, his mouth set in a grim line. "Why didn't you call me?"

"Because…"

"Because?" He needed to know why she didn't think she could count on him.

She sighed. "Because you'd think I was nothing but a klutz. You're always either rescuing me from spiders or mice or reading me the riot act for trying to paint a fire hydrant and—and…"

A klutz? She was a beautiful and capable woman. He intended to tell her so, but first he wanted to hear what else she had to say. "And what?"

"For once I want you to see me not as a charity case but as—as…" She sniffed.

He reached over, took her good hand in his and squeezed. "I don't see you as a klutz or a charity case. I admire you for taking on that house, adopting those kittens and coordinating the fundraiser."

"You're helping with the committee," she said, and he snorted but she ignored it and continued, "I haven't exactly succeeded with reopening the B and B."

"Yet. Anything else?"

"Yeah, that fire hydrant is still ugly as sin."

He shouted a laugh. "I'll get someone on it."

He started the Tacoma and pulled out of the parking spot. "I think we should stop and get the pain prescription filled."

She scowled. "I hate taking those."

"Better to have them," he said and headed for the pharmacy. "Loon Lake isn't exactly a twenty-four-hour town, so we should get them before it closes."

She grumbled but agreed. After the pharmacy he

drove her home. She'd assumed he was going to drop her off and go home, but he insisted on coming in and seeing her settled on the couch with her feet up.

"I broke my wrist, not my leg," she said, but had to admit it felt good to stretch out in her own home.

He grabbed a fleecy throw she'd left on one of the upholstered chairs and handed it to her.

"Do I look that bad?" she asked but accepted the throw.

"Yep."

"Hey."

"That's what you get for asking a silly question." He took the throw back, straightened it out with a snap and covered the bottom half of her body with it. "Where are they?"

She didn't even have to ask what he was talking about. "I put them in the playpen in the back room before I left but they're becoming escape artists, so I shut the pocket doors."

"I'll check on them. Would you like a cup of coffee or tea or something?"

"I can get…" She started to get up, but he pushed her back down.

"I'll get it." He leaned over her and kissed the top of her head.

She froze and noticed he had, too.

He straightened up and made a vague motion with his hand. "I, um…yeah."

"Okay," she said, not even sure what she was agreeing to.

He left the room—escaped, was more like it—and headed down the hall toward the back of the house. She sat in a daze, pulling the fleece throw back and forth through her fingers.

Why had that innocent gesture rattled her so?

In the kitchen, Cal filled her clear glass electric teakettle with water and turned it on. He turned around, leaned against the counter and stared off into space.

What the hell was that?

Sure, it was a friendly gesture but not something he could even conceive of doing with Ellie or Mary or Meg. He might give them a peck on the cheek. Or give Ellie a pretend smooch if he wanted to annoy Liam. This hadn't been any of those. Would Olive read anything into it? Did he want her to?

He slid open the pocket door to the family room, noticing that it needed a bit of finagling partway through to get it to open the rest of the way. He made a mental note to put that on the list of repairs.

So now you're keeping a list of repairs to her home?

Before he could argue with himself, two furry bundles scrambled toward him.

"Looks like the playpen isn't going to contain

you girls anymore, huh?" he asked as he hunkered down to pet them.

"Did they shred it or just climb over?"

He looked up at the sound of her voice. "I thought you were resting."

"I'm not an invalid."

"Maybe not, but you're my patient so at least take a seat at the table."

She looked like she might argue but eventually sighed and sank down in one of the chairs. Mayhem scurried over and tried to climb her leg, the kitten's claws digging into her jeans to gain traction.

Mischief raced across the kitchen floor, her claws making a clicking noise on the hardwood. She skidded to a stop, wiggled her butt and launched herself onto Olive's lap.

Olive caught the kitten before she could slip off and laughed. "Whoa. Did you see that?"

"I did. No wonder the playpen couldn't hold her."

Mayhem managed to climb her way onto Olive's lap and got into a tussle with her sister. They rolled around and both fell off despite Olive trying to prevent that.

He shook his head at their antics. "Are you hungry? I can run across the street and get that pizza I shoved into the fridge."

Olive wrinkled her nose. "I love pizza but how many days a week do you eat it?" Not waiting for an answer, she got up and went to her refrigerator.

"I have some leftover soup we can heat up."

She pointed to the covered containers, and he pulled them out. Setting one on the counter, he lifted the lid. "Vegetable soup?"

"*Pasta e fagioli.* Better known as pasta-and-bean soup. The recipe called for ground beef, but I used Italian sausage." She shook her head. "I really should learn to cook smaller portions."

"I'm not complaining. This looks delicious. Should I microwave it?"

She glanced at the water boiling in the electric kettle and he laughed. "Once I shut that off."

He prepared them each a cup of tea and set the soup in the microwave to reheat.

Once everything was done, he sat across from her at the table as the kittens batted miniature furry mice around the kitchen floor.

They talked about how well the tickets for the fundraiser had been selling.

"That's because you've been so dedicated to this," he told her. And that was the truth. He had worked to help her, but he feared he was the window dressing that Liam had warned her about.

"I feel really passionate about the camp."

He helped himself to more of the soup and refilled her bowl, too. "Because of your own background? Did you ever have any opportunities like what the Wilsons's camp offers?"

"No, but I understand what Mary wants for these

kids. I'm not saying that being in the system is a bad thing. A lot of at-risk children are rescued and helped by loving and caring families."

He got the impression she wanted to say more. In any other situation, with any other woman, he might have wanted to back away. Instead, he wanted to know more…like earlier, with learning she was left-handed. "But your experience wasn't always positive?"

As he spoke, he reached over and stroked the fingers sticking out of her cast.

"I was never abused or anything like that. As I got older, one of the things I hated the most was that my life was contained in a file that got passed around. As if my life was an open book and I didn't deserve the same amount of privacy that other people were allowed."

He hated the thought that this woman with the softest heart he'd ever encountered was treated like that. He wanted to go back in the past and demand that people in her life treat her with the respect she deserved. As much as he tried, he couldn't dismiss these feelings. He was growing close to her, closer than any other woman he'd known. That scared him, but no matter how much he tried to back off, he couldn't.

He was falling deeper and deeper into…what? He had no idea what he was falling into, nor did he know if he wanted it to stop.

* * *

Over Cal's objections, Olive helped him clean up after they finished their supper. She couldn't do a lot one-handed, but she did the best she could.

They sat in the family room with the kittens and let them run around and work off some energy.

"I guess if they can climb out of the playpen, I'll give them free rein in the house now and pray that what babyproofing I did will keep them out of trouble," she said and stifled a yawn.

"Why don't you go to bed. It's getting late and you need sleep to mend." He held up his hand as if knowing she might object. "I'll check around and make sure there's nothing they can get into."

"Are you sure?" She yawned again. She felt as if someone had suddenly unplugged her.

"Do you need help getting undressed?"

"Oh. I…no, I think I can manage it. I'll call down the stairs if I run into a problem."

"Good deal."

It was slow going and more than a bit frustrating, but she managed to undress and put on her nightgown. By the time she was done, she was dead on her feet.

She'd planned to go back downstairs after getting ready for bed, but just the thought was tiring. Before she could gather her strength, a light knock sounded at her door.

"Come in."

Cal popped his head around the door. "I just wanted to check on you."

She sighed in relief at not having to make a trip downstairs. "I confess I'm dead on my feet."

"Then get in bed. I'll take care of everything downstairs."

"Are you sure? I hate to impose. You've been such a help already."

"Get in bed and sleep," he ordered.

She yawned again. "But the kittens. They—"

"Don't worry about anything. And that includes Mischief and Mayhem. I've got this covered." He entered the room and threw back the covers on her bed. "Get in."

She did as he ordered only because she didn't have the strength to object. She crawled into bed and closed her eyes as he pulled the covers over her. That was the last thing she remembered.

Chapter Eleven

The next morning, Olive came slowly down the stairs and headed directly for the family room, next to the kitchen. She'd half expected the kittens to be clamoring for her to get up and wasn't sure if she should be concerned about their absence. Maybe Cal had gotten them to stay in the playpen.

She halted in the doorway at the sight that awaited her. Cal was sprawled in the recliner with one tabby kitten curled in a ball on his chest and another by his shoulder. All three were sound asleep.

He must have spent the night in that chair. Her heart expanded.

How could she not love this man?

She clapped a hand over her mouth to keep from vocalizing her discovery. What had she done?

You've fallen in love with Cal Pope. They'd only kissed once, but she couldn't deny her feelings any longer. She was head over heels for the wrong man— just the one thing she'd sworn to never do.

She slowly and silently backed out of the room with that accusation clanging inside her head. She needed time to collect herself and deal with that revelation. How could she have done something so foolish? Cal had made it perfectly clear that he wasn't a forever guy, and all she wanted was forever. In this house. *With him*, she admitted silently.

She wasn't so filled with hubris that she would think she could change his mind. Considering his background, she could understand his feelings. Understand, yes. Like them? No.

In the kitchen, she decided the least she could do was make him some breakfast. Scrambled eggs and toast couldn't be too difficult, even with only one hand.

"Famous last words," she muttered as she tried to figure out how to crack an egg with only one good hand.

"May I ask what you're doing?"

She startled at the voice in the doorway and took a step back, bumping into a small, furry body. Before she could stumble, Cal was behind her with a steadying hand.

"Thanks," she breathed and turned into his arms.

She looked up at him. His hair was even more disheveled than normal, his eyes had that just-woke-up look and there was sexy stubble on his chin and cheeks. Yeah, she was a goner.

"I—I was going to make breakfast. You didn't have to stay all night."

His gaze searched her face and she found herself wishing she'd applied makeup before coming downstairs.

"I wanted to be here if you needed me," he said.

"Thank you," she whispered.

He lowered his face to hers until she could feel his breath. What would that stubble feel like? Her lips parted in anticipation, but he frowned and took a step back, dropping his hands.

That was a good thing, she tried to tell herself, but disappointment was like a punch to the stomach.

"Sit," he told her. "I know how to scramble eggs."

"Then I'll make the toast." She couldn't just sit and watch him work in her kitchen.

In his stocking feet. Oh, God, why did that have to have that effect on her? She had to keep her hands busy, or she'd be reaching for him, so she pulled a loaf of bread out of the bread drawer.

"Can you believe it?" She closed the drawer with her hip.

"What?"

She laughed. "Nothing."

"Tell me."

"You'll think it's silly."

"Try me." He cracked eggs into the bowl she'd gotten out and began whipping them with a fork.

"I own a house with a kitchen that has a bread drawer."

He stopped his motions with the fork and raised an eyebrow at her. "You have a drawer that's especially for bread?"

"It's like a bread box inside a drawer." She knew she was blushing but couldn't help it. "I know. It's silly."

He grinned at her. "Then I must be even sillier because I'm jealous."

He got butter from the refrigerator and returned to the eggs. Adjusting the burner on the stove, he put the butter in the frying pan.

Standing with a spatula in one hand, he waited for the butter to melt.

She waited until he'd turned back to the stove and took the carton of eggs back out and set them on the table.

As the butter sizzled in the pan, she opened the carton. Just as she suspected.

"Is there a problem with the eggs?"

She quickly secured the cover on the carton of eggs. "Nope. Just putting them back into the refrigerator."

"I already did that. You took the carton back out and rearranged the eggs, didn't you?"

"Did I?" She tried to look innocent, but judging by the look on his face, she was failing…miserably.

"You don't like the way I removed them?" he asked.

"I didn't say that," she said.

"You didn't have to. Your actions spoke for you. You seem to have a problem with the way I handled the eggs." He quirked an eyebrow.

"Well, if you must know, you can't just remove them willy-nilly."

He frowned. "I can't?"

She shook her head. "You remove evenly from each end as you make your way to the middle."

His eyes widened in an exaggerated gesture. "So I've been doing it wrong all these years?"

"I wouldn't say wrong." She nibbled on the corner of her bottom lip.

"What would you say?"

"I'd say you're picking on me…again."

"And I'd say you're picking on *me*," he said, reaching for the carton. He took it from her and set it on the counter. "This is safer over here."

The look in those deep-set chocolate brown eyes forced her to swallow—twice—before she could ask why.

"Because I'm going to kiss you…unless you have an objection."

She shook her head. Nope. No objections. If she'd known talking about the placement of eggs in the carton was such a turn-on, she might have initiated it sooner.

He set down the spatula and removed the pan

from the burner before taking her face in both his hands. He touched his lips to hers.

She gasped as a jolt of pleasure ripped through her. The kiss was intimate, powerful, devastating. She—

"Ow," he said against her lips and pulled away.

"What? What's wrong?" She wanted to follow those lips with hers when he pulled back, but that was madness.

He winced. "I have a kitten trying to crawl up my leg."

She didn't know whether to be grateful or angry. "I need to start trimming their claws. Get them used to it."

He leaned down and carefully pulled the kitten claws from his pants. He held up the animal. "Blue eyes. Mayhem. Do you have any idea what you've interrupted?"

"I've been calling her May-May."

"And Mischief is?"

"Missy, and she's trying to climb your other leg."

He shook his head, looking exasperated but not angry. "You'd think since I bought them one of those cat-climbing trees, they'd leave me alone?"

She laughed. "Not possible. You're too irresistible."

He leaned over and pressed his lips to hers again, lightly this time, but the kitten began batting their faces and Olive got a case of the giggles.

Cal pulled the kitten away from his face and scolded the creature. "You're a failure as a wingman."

"I wouldn't say that," Olive said, remembering the evening he showed up with the kittens. If she'd been teetering on the edge of falling in love with Cal before that, the sight of him at her door with those balls of fluff and knowing that he'd rescued them had pushed her over the edge. Of course, by that time, it wouldn't have taken much more than a tap on the shoulder to push her over.

Damn. In love. No, she couldn't be. Shouldn't be.

"What is it? What's wrong?" He frowned when she stepped back.

I've fallen in love with you. No, she couldn't admit that. Not now. *Not ever.*

Cooking breakfast with two kittens underfoot wasn't the easiest but they managed.

"I see now how your accident happened," he said as he dug into his eggs and buttered a slice of toast, which he handed to her.

"My accident?" She frowned. Had she missed something? Her mind was still processing her feelings for him. She had to avoid blurting out how she felt about him.

He paused with a forkful of scrambled eggs partway to his mouth: "Tripping over Mischief."

"Mayhem," she corrected, wrinkled her forehead, and chuckled. "At least I think it was. And that reminds me... I called the vet office today to inquire about having them spayed and was informed that half the bill had been paid in advance. What's that all about?"

He shrugged and ate the last bites of his eggs and pointed to her almost-empty plate. "Want more?"

"No, but I do want you to tell me why you did that."

"How do you know it was me?"

She rolled her eyes at him. "Why did you do that?"

"I dumped them on you, so it was the least I could do," he said and held up his hand before she could protest. "I feel partially responsible."

"But you didn't trip."

He grinned and touched his fingertip to the end of her nose. "This isn't about that. It's about how I thrusted pet ownership onto you."

She swallowed twice for fear she might start drooling. That's how much he wrecked her when he touched her. "I...I could have refused."

He reached down and picked up a kitten, glancing between her and the kitten.

"Okay. You've made your point. Thank you. For both." She finished her eggs and last bite of toast.

"You're not planning on going into work today, are you? A broken wrist deserves at least a day off."

"Yeah. I have a feeling it may take me a while to shower and get dressed." She sighed.

"Want some help?" He wiggled his eyebrows as he gathered up the dishes.

"As a matter of fact..."

He brought their dirty dishes to the sink and swiveled back around, a comically expectant expression on his face.

"I could use help securing a plastic bag to the cast, so I don't get it wet." She bit her lower lip to keep from laughing.

"Tease," he muttered, but was grinning.

After he helped her tape a bag over the cast, he told her he was running home to shower and change clothes.

"It's fine. I don't need a babysitter."

"I'm not babysitting, Olive. I'm helping a friend."

"Thank you," she said and meant it.

But that didn't mean she wasn't conflicted over being labeled a friend. She did want to be his friend. The fact she longed for more was her problem, not his. And remaining friends was important because she didn't want to jeopardize her relationships with the others they called friends.

While Olive was in the shower, Cal walked back to his place and called Liam to tell him he was taking a vacation day. He explained what had happened and endured the short silence at the other end of the call.

"And you want to be there for her?" Liam asked.

Cal rolled his eyes. "I'm being neighborly."

"Uh-huh."

Cal ground his teeth. "She lives across the street."

"Uh-huh."

"She's a friend."

"Uh-huh."

"Are you good with my time off?" Cal demanded.

"Yeah. Go ahead. You deserve it. And say hi to Olive for me."

Cal gave him an anatomically impossible instruction and hung up in the middle of Liam's laughter.

After showering and shaving, he went back to Olive's place. He wanted to be sure she was able to shower and get dressed.

He found her in the family room with the kittens.

"You need help getting the bag off?"

She shrugged. "I guess."

"What's wrong?"

"I was able to shower but I couldn't wash my hair. I called Colleen's Cut and Caboodle in town, but they're booked up."

"And you need to wash your hair?"

"Yeah." She lifted it with her uninjured hand and let it fall back down as if it was obvious.

It looked fine to him, but he'd been around Ellie long enough to know not to say that.

"Sorry. I get cranky when my hair is dirty."

Again, he wasn't going to argue. "Do you want me to wash it?"

What? No! He did not just offer to wash her hair.

"You'd be willing to do that for me?"

Absolutely not. Uh-uh. No way. "I've never washed

anyone else's before but I do wash mine, so I guess you could say I've had practice."

Her face brightened. "Thank you. You're a sweetheart."

"Yeah, let's keep that just between us."

"Of course." She bounced out of the chair. "I'll get shampoo and a towel."

After she'd left the room, he glared at the kittens. He could have sworn they were doing the cat equivalent of laughing. He growled at them, and they fell over one another in their haste to scurry away.

His stomach knotted. *Great. Nothing like taking your frustrations out on innocent kittens.*

"Girls. C'mon back here."

He and the kittens had made up by the time Olive returned with towels, bottles and a hairbrush. Too bad all relationship problems couldn't be solved by rolling a balled-up piece of aluminum foil across the floor.

"What are you grinning at?" she asked.

"Them," he said, and it was the truth. Sort of.

Her eyes went all soft and tender as she looked at them. "When you first brought them, I confess I was skeptical, but now I can't imagine how lonely this place would feel without them. Thank you."

He had difficulty swallowing. *It's because of allergy season*, he told himself. The tightness in his throat had nothing to do with that look in her eyes. *Nope. Allergies.*

"I was thinking the kitchen sink might be best since it has a spray nozzle," she said, breaking the silence.

He blinked. "Kitchen sink?"

"My hair?"

"Oh, yeah. That."

She peered up at him. "You haven't changed your mind, have you?"

"And risk your wrath?" He puckered his lips and made a face. "I know how cranky you get when you can't wash your hair."

She laughed and tossed a towel at him. "Better believe it, mister."

He caught the towel and shook it out. The kittens sat staring up at them, their little heads ping-ponging from one to the other.

He pointed a finger at them. "Behave or you're next."

Mayhem sneezed and shook her head. Her sister seized the opportunity and jumped on her, and they rolled around on the floor, wrapped around one another in a feline version of wrestling.

Their antics had helped the tension building in him, but his hands were still sweaty as he followed her to the kitchen.

Olive inhaled as she sat in the chair he'd pulled up to the sink. This had sounded like a good idea after the disappointment of not being able to go to the salon until next week.

And he'd offered, right? she tried reassuring herself.

He turned on the water and began wetting her hair. He stood so close that if she turned her head even a smidgen, she could bury her face in those abs. Would they feel as hard as they looked?

She couldn't prevent the moan from escaping as he massaged the shampoo into her scalp. Having someone wash your hair was a pleasure, but she'd never reacted like this before.

By the time he was rinsing the shampoo out of her hair, his shirt had some water splotches on it. Hmm, maybe she should have suggested he take off his shirt.

She sighed and he stopped. "Everything okay?"

"Yes. Fine." *I was just fantasizing about your stomach.*

Face it, Olive, you were thinking about things a bit lower, too.

She groaned.

"I'm almost done. Is your wrist bothering you?"

"It hurts every once in a while." Which wasn't *exactly* a lie. But pretty close, she admonished herself.

"Done," he said and reached for a towel.

He wrapped the cloth around her hair and squeezed. "I can do the rest. You must already be late for work."

"I had some vacation days due me."

"And you wasted them on me?"

He set the wet towel on the counter and picked up a hairbrush. "I'm not wasting them."

And she thought him washing her hair was decadent. Having him brush it was even more so.

"What are those?" he asked, pointing the brush at three small wooden houses on the top of her refrigerator.

"Bird feeders. I ordered them online, but I haven't had a chance to hang them up outside."

"And you won't…at least not for a while."

"Four to six weeks, unless I figure out a way to do it one-handed."

"Show me where you want them, and I'll do it."

"I didn't mean for you to do it for me. I need to be independent, and you keep coming to my rescue. This is my house." She resisted the urge to stamp her foot. Yeah, that would go a long way toward him seeing her as an adult.

He quirked an eyebrow. "You'd rather let those poor birds go hungry?"

"That's not fair. They've survived this long without my feeders, I'm sure they can make it for another two months."

He tutted his tongue. "You're beginning to sound cynical."

"Maybe you're rubbing off on me," she teased.

"I hope not, because I like the weed-loving, plant-rescuing Olive."

And right then and there, her heart melted. Again.

How was she ever going to be able to resist him if she spent time with him? Thank goodness the last big thing they needed to do for the fundraiser was to attend the Coffee & Conversation meeting at the library to ask for their help in selling the raffle tickets.

After all this was over, she'd go back to seeing Cal when he would wave from across the street and they'd smile and chat when they got together with their group of friends.

Yeah, that would happen. She'd learn how to stop being in love with him. Failing that, she'd learn to live with this knife edge of emotion being around him caused.

Cal eased his official Loon Lake FD vehicle into a tight spot in the library's parking lot. He'd called Olive earlier in the day to explain he'd had to travel to the state capital, so he'd have to come straight to the meeting.

He frowned as he glanced around at the parked cars and didn't see Olive's. Maybe someone had given her a ride. Although the doctor had given her the okay to drive, she was cautious because of the cast.

"You and Olive haven't had a tiff, have you?"

Cal ground his molars. This was the third person to ask the same damn question since he'd walked into the library's community room. He'd had to come to tonight's meeting straight from work, so he had no idea why Olive was a no-show because when he'd tried to call her to say he was running late his call had gone directly to voice mail.

Going to this monthly meeting had been her idea. Some locals met every month to discuss ways to give a little extra help to town residents who might be in need. They'd organized their meals to even include pet food for a recipient's animals.

Cal glanced at the laminated sign that said Coffee & Conversation. According to the librarian, Addie Bishop, the name alternated between months. She'd laughed and explained that some months it was Tea & Talk, then whispered that it really should be called Drinks & Drama. Having grown up in town, he knew that small-town life could be a double-edged sword. People had your back in times of trouble but liked nothing better than to haggle over the details and to spread gossip.

"I don't know why she's not here," Cal told the person who'd asked. He knew she worked for the local insurance agent, but he couldn't remember her name.

"I'm sure she had a good reason. Olive is a very dependable person," said Ogle, Tavie's husband, who'd sauntered over and handed Cal a cup of coffee.

"Yeah, right." Cal snorted, but immediately regretted it. Ogle was right. Olive wasn't the type to just blow any of this off. She'd taken this whole thing seriously.

His phone dinged and he checked the text message. It was from Olive, and he breathed a sigh of relief. At least she was alive. His imagination had been overactive for the past half hour.

He frowned as he read the text.

Sorry. Not coming.

That was it? That's all the explanation she was giving him. He texted back.

Why not?

His first reaction was to leave and go to Olive, if nothing but to reassure himself that she was okay. But Addie had called the meeting to order and was introducing him, so he was trapped.

He explained to those gathered that he and Olive had planned on a raffle to raise funds to help defray the cost of constructing another bunkhouse at Camp Life Launch. The camp had reached capacity and was having to turn away some kids.

He explained that they'd secured a grand prize of a weekend in Boston, but they wanted some lesser prizes. Olive had thought people at this meeting might be willing to donate a prize or know someone who would.

If Olive had been here, she'd have done a much better job of convincing people. He sat back down and checked his phone to see if she'd responded to his text demanding an explanation.

Addie leaned toward him and said, "Look, Cal, if you want to cut out early and check on Olive, I can take over from here. We've covered most everything, anyway."

"Thanks. I—"

"Go," everyone said in unison.

Fifteen minutes later, he pulled his truck into her driveway. There were lights blazing in the Victorian, so he knew she was home. Was she ill? After leaving the meeting, he'd asked her via text if everything was okay and she'd assured him she was fine but couldn't make the occasion.

"You better have a good reason for all this," he muttered and slammed out of his vehicle.

Something's come up was all the explanation he'd gotten. He'd had to face all those people by himself. She'd been the one with all the big ideas and he couldn't remember a damn one, because his brain was occupied with worrying about her. This was why he didn't do relationships. You trusted people and they let you down.

He stomped up the porch steps. He glanced at the antique Victorian twist doorbell and decided to skip it. The way he was feeling he might end up breaking it. It would serve her right, but something held him back.

He pounded on the door and shouted her name. She was the one with all the notebooks full of lists and spreadsheets and who knew what else. He'd told her he couldn't run the damn thing and she'd assured him she'd be there. So much for being able to depend on her. He was right to mistrust people. They always let you down when push came to—

She opened the door, and all thoughts flew out of his head.

"I'm sorry. I shouldn't have..." Olive immediately began to apologize as he glared at her.

He narrowed his eyes when her voice trailed off, as if finishing the sentence was beyond her. What the...? His anger evaporated and was replaced with concern. "What's wrong? Are you sick?"

She shook her head and turned away, heading down the hallway.

"Olive. What's wrong? I deserve an explanation," he demanded.

She felt ashamed, guilty and annoyed, all at once. She should have known he'd come here after the meeting. Did she secretly want him to come? Is that why she'd been so cryptic with her text?

"I told you I—" she protested feebly.

"You told me squat." He scowled at her.

"I sent you a text message." A lousy text message when she owed him a thorough explanation.

"A text that said you were sorry you couldn't make the meeting."

"It was the truth. I couldn't come to the meeting," Olive said. She couldn't face all those people. Most were her friends, and they would have known something was wrong.

"Why not?"

"It's personal and—"

"What happened, Olive?"

She sighed deeply. How could she explain this to him when she barely understood it herself? She was over Kurt. Over their broken engagement. She wasn't still hung up on it, pining for the fiancé she'd lost. So why did this news hurt so much? It was irrational. As was her bursting into tears when she'd followed the link someone had sent her.

But then, emotions weren't always rational. *Such as you falling in love with Cal.*

"You wouldn't understand."

"Try me."

She pulled her phone out of her pocket and clicked on the pictures of a beaming Kurt and his wife announcing the birth of their son. She held up the phone, expecting him to dismiss her feelings or tell her she was being unreasonable once he examined what was on the screen. Because she was. She shouldn't care what her ex and his wife were doing. It shouldn't matter. If she'd been a good person, she'd be happy for them. Wouldn't she?

"You're still in love with your ex?" He looked flabbergasted and sad, and she couldn't handle the emotions warring on his face.

"No," she quickly assured him. "That's the odd part. I realized after we broke off the engagement that I hadn't been in love…not truly in love. I loved the idea of being a couple and suddenly I had this extended family, thanks to him. I was in love with the concept of being a couple."

"Then, I'm not sure I understand."

"I'm not sure I do, either, but it hurt when I saw those pictures. I kept wondering why it was always happening to other people and not me." Why couldn't she attract some of that energy or whatever it was that drew people to others?

"In this day and age, you don't need to be married to have a baby," he told her. "Hell, you don't even need a father in the picture to have a baby. You know all that, Olive."

"Of course, I know all of that." She sighed. "I can't explain my reaction."

He took her hands in his and led her over to the couch, where they sat, and he rubbed her back. "I think it's normal to feel jealous or sad or whatever when you see other people getting what you want."

"But—"

He put his finger over her lips. "No *buts*. I'm not here to judge you."

"I let you down by not being there tonight. That—

that was selfish of me." She felt miserable letting him down, but she hadn't been able to see past her pain. She'd been afraid she might start crying and embarrass herself in front of the people gathered for the meeting.

She turned to him and melted when she saw the genuine concern in his eyes. She couldn't keep the catch from her voice. "Cal?"

She leaned forward and when he didn't move away, she had the courage to touch her lips to his. He let her explore. If not for his shallow breaths, she might have thought he was simply enduring her explorations.

"Where are the hellions?" he asked, glancing around.

She frowned, thinking he didn't want the same thing she did. But he shook his head, as if reading her mind.

"I don't want them interrupting," he explained.

"They're still recovering from yesterday's spay procedures, so I put them in the playpen to sleep. The collars have deterred them from climbing out. The vet said to curtail their activities for a couple days."

He tucked a stray curl behind her ear. "Olive, are you sure about this? I don't want to take advantage of you."

"You don't want me?" Oh, God. What had she done?

"Believe me, I want you. I want you more than you can imagine."

His words had reassured her, but she still needed to be sure. "Then why the reluctance?"

He searched her face, needing to be sure. Taking advantage of the vulnerability caused by her ex was the last thing he wanted. "If we go through with this tonight, now, it isn't going to change my mind about commitment." There. He'd said it. Put the one thing on the table.

"How about we go upstairs to the bedroom?" She reached up for him and he forgot everything else.

Holding hands, they raced up the stairs.

In her bedroom, he stood in front of her and slipped his hands under her shirt. He moaned when his exploring fingers encountered lace, a tiny scrap of lace.

She frowned. "What?"

"You're wearing lacy underwear."

"You like that?"

"What color are they?"

"Pink. Why? Does it matter?"

He chuckled. "They could be plain white cotton for all I care."

She frowned. "And here I thought you'd be a pink-lace kind of guy."

"You bought them for me?"

"Well, I bought them for *me* but with you in mind."

He opened his mouth but all he could manage was a moan.

"You're killing me, sweetheart," he whispered. "Now it's my turn to make you moan."

He lifted her shirt and began easing the arm with the cast out of the sleeve. "I'll try not to hurt you, but it's a bit awkward."

She pulled her arm out of the sleeve and helped him get the shirt off.

After tossing aside the shirt, he twined his fingers in her hair, fisted his hand and gave it a gentle tug. He was doing this to her, but the action sent sparks zipping through *him*.

"I've wanted to do that for the longest time," he admitted.

"And I've imagined you doing just that," she countered in a breathless tone.

He groaned and kissed her, losing himself in the glory that was her mouth as he eased them toward the bed. He'd told her the truth about wanting his hands in her hair, and now he wanted them all over her. He didn't want to leave a spot untouched, by his fingers or his tongue.

He laid her on the bed and followed, never breaking contact with her lips. He moved so they were lying face-to-face and cupped her breasts in his palms. They were perfect.

She made a sound in her throat, and he squeezed with one hand and reached around with the other and unclasped her bra. He kissed and sucked as he eased it off.

"And what have we here?"

Her hand flew up, covering a small mole—not much more than a dot—on the slope of her left breast.

"It's nothing to be ashamed of," he growled and pushed her hand away, touching the spot with the tip of his tongue.

"Please," she groaned, the sound zipping straight to his groin.

"Please what?" he asked, lifting his head from her breast.

"I want more."

"Then you shall have more," he said and unsnapped her jeans and eased the zipper down as he rained kisses over her stomach. She helped him by shimmying out of the pants.

He groaned and put his hands on her hips and rubbed his thumbs along the lace.

"So beautiful," he whispered and kissed the skin above the waistband, drawing his tongue across the top, savoring the soft, silky skin.

Chapter Twelve

Olive looked down at Cal, his head bent over her stomach. The dark hair in the shadowed hollow of his neck brought tears to her eyes. As much as she'd tried to talk herself out of having sex with him, she couldn't. She was helplessly, hopelessly in love. Oh sure, she might yearn for more, but if passionate sex was all she was getting, she'd take it. She deserved to be selfish once in a while.

He ran his fingers over her thighs and around her hip. "You have delicious curves, Olive. So sexy. So beautiful."

"And you have too many clothes on," she told him.

"I can fix that." He stood and stripped with more speed than finesse.

He stretched out beside her and kissed her, working his way across her cheek. She arched her head back as he nibbled on her earlobe and ran his tongue along a spot under her ear.

When she moaned, he smiled against her damp skin. "You like that?"

"Mmm," she murmured, lost in the sensations he was creating.

"You do things to me. I've never wanted another woman like I've wanted you," he said hoarsely.

He groaned and his leg pushed her thighs open but brought his face level with hers again. His tongue pressed against the seam of her lips, demanding entry. She opened her mouth and his tongue thrust in, dueling with hers. All thoughts flew out of her head.

His arousal pressed against her stomach. She reached down to touch it and his hips bucked toward her. She had longed for this moment, longed for him. She refused to let thoughts of the future or commitment get in the way of her enjoyment of their lovemaking.

He reached between their bodies and cupped his palm around her sex, and he slipped a finger inside, while his thumb stroked her nub. All her nerve endings hummed and sizzled as his calloused finger and thumb drove her to the edge.

She cried out in frustration when he pulled his hand away.

"Cal…" She heard the desperation in her own voice.

"Patience," he said and kissed her. "I want to make this last. I've been dreaming of this since I first laid eyes on you. Will you let me taste you?"

"We must have shared the same dreams," she confessed.

Spreading her legs, he licked the sensitive flesh on her inner thighs. She shook her head and cried in frustration. She grabbed his head between her hands and tried to guide him to the part of her that ached for his touch. When his mouth finally found that spot, she cried out and dug her fingers into his scalp.

But he had other ideas and he controlled the pace, bringing her to the edge, then easing up.

"Oh, please," she begged when he touched her again. "Yes, right there."

He applied a little more pressure, and she came apart in his hand.

"I was hoping you'd be inside me when that happened."

He scooted up and scooped up his pants, digging his wallet out of a pocket. He pulled out a cellophane packet and fumbled until he got it open.

"May I?" she asked as he started to sheath himself.

Her hands shook as she rolled the condom in place, taking her sweet time, torturing and teasing as he hissed through his teeth.

"Enough. I can't hold out much longer." He positioned himself at her entrance. "Tell me to stop if it hurts and I will."

"It's okay. I want you. Now."

He thrust into her and stopped, as if savoring the moment. At least that's what she assumed because that's what she was doing, savoring this first moment when they were one. Once he started to move in and out, she lifted her legs, crossing her heels around the small of his back. Reaching toward the peak again, she urged him to keep up his pace.

As soon as she cried out, he thrust one last time and shuddered as his release hit him.

He stretched out next to her and anchored her against him with his arm, taking care with her right arm. She rested her head on his chest.

"That was amazing." She caressed his chest, enjoying the feel of the crisp hairs against her palm. She pressed a kiss to his skin and enjoyed the tang of salt from his sweat. "Was it good for you, too?"

"Amazing," he echoed and kissed the top of her head.

She was lying in his arms, reveling in what had just happened. Refusing to think beyond this moment. The future would come soon enough. She'd borne heartache in the past, she'd bear it again.

"No matter what happens in the future, I—"

"Olive, please. I—"

"No. Let me say this." Before she chickened out. "I want you to know I'm not going to regret this."

"Neither will I," he said, brushing the hair back from her forehead.

His tender gesture gave her the courage to continue. "I will always be grateful for this fabulous home and for the healing I've found in Loon Lake. But most of all for you."

"I'm glad you fit me in there somewhere." He gave her a mock frown.

She danced her fingers across his abs. "I saved the best for last."

"In that case, I'm glad I came back after the air force," he said and settled her against his side.

"Why did you leave the military? You must have had quite a bit of time in." She wanted to know as much as possible about the man she'd not only given her body to but also her heart.

Cal sighed and rubbed his fingertips along her arm. Normally, he didn't talk much about his reasons for joining and ultimately leaving the air force, but he didn't mind telling her.

Must have been the mind-blowing sex, he mused.

"What made you leave?" she asked again and shifted closer, all that glorious hair brushing against his arm. "From what you've said, you found satisfaction in your work."

"I did and then I didn't."

"What happened?" She rubbed the knuckles of her good hand over his chest.

"Politicians."

Lifting her head, she frowned. "What do you mean?"

"Politics sometimes got in the way of who we were able to rescue and who we weren't."

She gave him a puzzled frown. "I thought you rescued whoever needed rescuing."

"It didn't always work like that." If only it had. He might still be there. Hmm, but then he'd have missed out on this.

She remained silent, probably waiting for him to elaborate. He appreciated that she didn't prod but let him decide if he wanted to tell her more.

"We got a call about a boy who'd had his leg blown off in an open-air marketplace. We were all set to go when we were told to stand down. We weren't allowed to go and help."

"I don't understand."

"Believe me, we didn't like it any better but those were our orders and we had to set aside personal feelings."

She sighed. "That must've been hard."

"I think that's when I started to question what I was doing. We never got emotionally involved with any of the soldiers we rescued. They were packages and we were the delivery method. I know that sounds crass but it's the way it had to be. We did our jobs and if we did it right and were lucky and got them back to the hospital at Bagram, Afghanistan, before that golden hour expired, then they lived. But whatever the outcome, we'd done our jobs. But this—" he swallowed the bile rising in his throat "—this was a child. Some of the other guys had kids of their own and it took a toll on them."

"I'm so sorry. That really sucks."

He appreciated that she didn't give him any of the tired platitudes he was accustomed to. But then, Olive wasn't like anyone else he'd ever met. He certainly wouldn't have considered saying any of this stuff to any of the other women he'd slept with. He just wouldn't. And yet, here he was, practically pouring his heart out.

He swallowed. What was he doing?

"Do you miss being a PJ?" she asked before he could follow through on that thought.

He decided answering her question was easier than contemplating his complicated feelings about her.

"Sometimes." He thought of the way Tavie had given him guff over the fire-code violations. "I miss the guys. Your teammates become like family. But I don't miss having to maintain that macho image."

"What do you mean?"

"Well, for instance, our team was stateside and had been out partying. We got stopped by the cops on the way back to base. We ended up getting arrested because we acted like jerks." He laughed. "Real jerks. We weren't going to let anyone, not even the police, push us around or give us orders."

"So, what happened?"

"We had to call our CO—that's commanding officer—and he came and got us released. Of course, that meant he meted out the punishment." He chuckled. "We might have been better off with the cops."

"You didn't get into big trouble, did you?"

"Nah. He was used to attitude from the PJs. The attrition rate during training is astronomical, so you have to have a healthy ego to make it through."

"I guess if they expect you to run into a burning building or into the heat of battle to rescue wounded soldiers, they have to expect some attitude."

"Exactly!" He appreciated the fact she understood and didn't assume he was just full of himself. It was a necessary mind game.

"But you left that behind when you left the air force? Is that something you can turn off?"

He shrugged. "I guess when you're not around the other guys, it's easier to shut some of it down."

He had worked on rounding some of his sharp edges after he came home to Loon Lake. Liam had helped him get on with the fire department, so he once again had a team of guys who had his back. There wasn't as much swagger in the guys in the department as there had been with the PJs, but they were a great group. He got along with them and after they'd taken him down a peg, they'd accepted him.

He grinned at the memories of the first few weeks, when they'd let him know he wasn't a PJ anymore and they wouldn't stand for any posturing.

That was probably a good thing because Olive might not have been as attracted to that guy with the giant ego. And he definitely wanted her attracted.

With his hand under her chin, he lifted her face to his and kissed her.

Reluctantly pulling away, he asked, "I don't suppose you happen to have any condoms lying around this place?"

Despite the lust glittering in her eyes, she blushed. "Sadly no." She licked her lips. "But maybe we could experiment with some…um…"

"Alternatives?" He grinned at how deeply she was blushing despite what they'd just done. "I like your thought process, Olive Downing."

Olive woke up with a smile on her face and an arm across her waist. An arm that didn't belong to her.

She edged closer to the end of the mattress, intending to slip away to answer the call of nature. But Cal grumbled and pulled her closer.

"Where do you think you're going?" he asked in a voice thick from sleep.

"I need to use the bathroom."

He grunted and released her. By the time she returned, he was sitting up in bed, yawning and running his hand through his bedhead hair.

She tied the robe she'd thrown on in the bathroom. "I don't know about you, but I'm hungry."

He swung out of bed and marched toward her, seemingly unconcerned about his nakedness.

"I thought you said you didn't have any condoms." He pulled her into his arms, growled and nuzzled her neck.

"I meant food," she said in a breathless tone.

"It's the middle of the night. I doubt we can get a pizza at this hour." He kissed the spot where her neck and shoulder met.

"I have some homemade soup I can heat up." What did that say about her that she had leftover soup but no condoms? She'd be more prepared next time.

Whoa. Who said there'd be a next time?

"What's wrong?" He gave her a curious look.

"Is that all you eat? Pizza?"

"Not since this woman moved in across the street and, for some reason, always has leftovers. I know she must cook but all she talks about are the leftovers."

She playfully hit his shoulder. "Do you want me to bring it up here or do you want to eat in the kitchen?"

He glanced at the bed with its tangled sheets. "Kitchen. This room is too tempting."

"I'll heat up the soup while you get dressed."

He frowned. "Your kitchen isn't clothing optional?"

She smirked. "It is, but you might not want to risk kitten claws in your lap. I'm just saying."

His hand covered a part of his anatomy in what looked like an automatic reaction. "You've made your point."

In the kitchen she put some soup in a pan on the stove to heat up and some dry kibble in the kittens' bowls. They seemed excited about the midnight snack.

He came in the kitchen as she was dishing out the soup. As soon as Cal sat down, Mischief wiggled her butt and attempted to jump into his lap. She didn't quite make it, but he grabbed her and helped her up. He gave her some loving, then put her back on the floor so he could eat. She trotted off and began wrestling with her sister.

"This soup is delicious," he said as he began to eat. "Where did you learn to cook?"

"I took some online culinary video classes." She set her spoon down. "Did your mom like to cook?"

"Some." He shrugged. "After my dad left, my nana kept us fed…among other things."

"Your nana?"

"My maternal grandmother came to live with us, and she basically pulled us through. My mom never fully recovered but my nana stepped in. If not for her, I don't know where I'd have ended up. After my dad left, I let my grades slip but she made sure I finished high school at least. College was out by then but I entered the air force instead."

"Had you planned on college?" Her life had been

turned upside down by the death of her parents, but she'd managed to recover before putting her future in jeopardy.

"Yeah, but Dear Old Dad also wiped out my college fund when he left."

"That's terrible." She brought her hand up to cover her mouth. She didn't want to dent his pride by fussing over him. But knowledge didn't change the fact she wanted to hold him and stroke him as if he were a child.

He shrugged. "It's my own fault. Not attending classes, I mean. I let my grades slip for a bit in high school so any chances of getting a scholarship was out."

"But you made up for it in the air force. I looked it up and I know the attrition rate for pararescue training is eighty percent. So, Cal Pope, consider yourself a superhero.

"Your poor mother. But I guess when the man you love, and trust, does something—"

"Love and trust didn't enter into it." He shook his head. "My mother liked her position in the community. She enjoyed being the wife of Oscar Pope and living in the large house. And, yes, I understand how humiliating the whole situation was for her, but it was for me, too. I guess we were both selfish, huh?"

"What? No. Absolutely not. You were a child. It's about the only time in your life when you can be selfish."

"I was mad at my dad, not for leaving, but get this, I was mad at him for leaving me behind." He made a noise in his throat. "But then, what guy runs off with a younger woman and takes a teenager with him?"

She had no idea what to say to him. Pointing out that when you're running off with your much younger secretary, taking your teen son with you probably isn't a likely option would be gauche. And as much as she wanted to comfort him, she wasn't sure what to say. She hadn't felt this helpless since those dreary early days in foster care.

"I wish I could have been there to comfort you and help you, so you didn't have to carry the burden alone."

Maybe she shouldn't have admitted so much, but she couldn't contain it any longer. Besides, he'd helped her wash her hair. No guy interested in casual or intending to cut and run would have been so thoughtful. Would he?

Afraid of letting her thoughts out, she said the first thing that came to her. "You have every right to your feelings after what your dad did."

"My feelings?" Cal couldn't stop the bitterness rising in him. "I have no idea what I'm supposed to feel about him now. I haven't a clue where he is. Is he still with *her*?" He practically spit the word. "Is he still alive?"

"I always thought I had it bad but at least I know

where my dad is. There's a grave I can visit if I feel the need. Oh, my God, I'm sorry." Her hand flew up to cover her mouth. "That sounded terrible. I didn't mean—"

"It's okay, I understand. Truly." He felt some of the bitterness evaporating. As if admitting it to her had freed him from its embrace.

"No. I shouldn't have said something like that," she fretted.

He took her good hand in his two. "Talking to you was good. I needed to let some of that out."

"Yeah, it's not good to hold stuff in."

And that's what he'd been doing for a long time. She had helped him feel better. Maybe he could return the favor.

Chapter Thirteen

"What about you, Olive?" he urged as he helped her clear away the dirty dishes from their midnight snack.

"Tell me about your childhood." He had never wanted to dig below the surface of other women he'd slept with. Keep Things Casual was his motto. Until now. Until Olive. Why was she so different?

She shrugged. "It was pretty normal up until my parents died."

He took the dirty pan out of her hand and set it in the sink and tucked her close to him. He led her into the family room, the kittens at their heels. "Do you remember much about your biological parents?"

"I remember a few snatches here and there, but I can't always tell what's a true memory or something I'd dreamed of or wished had happened. Added to that, every year the memories fade a little more."

"Have you ever written them down?"

Her eyes widened. "Oh, my God, how did you know? My last foster mother before I aged out encouraged me to write them down. I only wish I had started sooner...when they were fresher."

"Tell me a memory," he urged.

"Whenever I lavender, I think of my mom. I remember sitting on her bed watching her get dressed to go out somewhere and she spritzed on some perfume. She sprayed a small amount on me, too. She said it would be like me having her with me that night."

"And now you smell like lavender."

She pulled away enough to look at him. "You noticed that?"

"I've noticed a lot of things about you," he said, knowing it was true.

Where had this woman been all his life? If he had met her before getting taken in by that journalist who'd pretended to care, he would have immediately seen the difference between genuine affection and false declarations.

"C'mon, it's late. We both need a good night's sleep," he said.

They walked up the stairs to her bedroom. They slipped back into bed and he made a mental note to be sure to pick up a pack of condoms.

Chapter Fourteen

"Hey, Cal, see you around six?"

Cal looked up from the report he was typing into his computer on the desk in his office. Colton Jensen was leaning against the doorjamb. Colton was an EMT and friend Cal sometimes met for a beer and to shoot the breeze. Although he hadn't spoken with Colton lately. Cal and Olive had been spending most of their free time together.

"Yo, Cal, we good for tonight?"

As Cal continued to stare at him, Colton shook his head and clucked his tongue. "Don't tell me you've been so caught up with that woman you've been seeing that you forgot about it."

Cal wracked his brain. The poker game! Colton

had told him he'd get him in the next time he and the guys got together. How could he have forgotten that? "Hey, just messing with you. I'll be there."

After Colton left the firehouse, Cal stared unseeing at the report he'd been working on. Had he gotten so wrapped up in Olive that he'd forsaken everything else? It had been a month since they'd first made love—yeah, he was calling it that. He hadn't moved in or anything, but they spent many evenings together working on renovations to the Victorian and watching the kittens grow.

Was he in a relationship?

Yeah, he was. He'd spent all his time with her. He swallowed. Not only that, but he'd also confided secrets to her…about his feelings about his dad not taking him when he left, about his reasons for leaving the military.

After a month of togetherness, what was Olive expecting from him? Did she think they were in a relationship? He hated the thought that he could possibly hurt her, but great sex didn't mean he was automatically ready to commit.

He'd warned her he didn't do commitment and she'd accepted. Olive was too honest and open to try to manipulate him using sex. This was on him. He was the one sending mixed signals with stuff like washing her hair.

He reached for his phone. He'd better call her and let her know he wouldn't be around for supper. No matter what, he couldn't just blow her off tonight without even an explanation.

"Sunshine Gardens. Olive speaking. May I help you?"

His mouth went dry when he heard her voice. He had forgotten about the game. His mind had been filled with Olive. It was as if he'd been in a relationship, part of a couple. As much time as he spent with her, he refused to call it anything other than friends hanging out. Yeah, okay, friends with benefits, but still…

How the hell had that happened? When had it happened? And more importantly, how had he let it?

"Hello? Anybody there?"

Olive's voice jolted him from his spiraling thoughts. "Olive?"

"Cal? What's wrong?"

Everything. "I, uh, I wanted to let you know I won't be around tonight. You hadn't planned anything, did you?"

"Well, I…no, I guess not. It's just that we usually watch movies on Friday night."

He heard the hurt and confusion in her voice and wanted to kick himself. They had a routine. Couples had routines. How had he let things get so out of his control?

At the end of the day, instead of going to the poker game, he made an excuse to Colton, endured good-natured razzing and headed home.

No. Not home, he corrected himself. The Victorian wasn't his home, even if he'd spent more time there in the past month than at his own place.

He drew his hand across his brow to wipe away sweat that had gathered there. Slowing his truck, he glanced between his place and Olive's and drove into his own driveway.

"Making a statement?" he asked as he jumped out of the pickup.

"Some statement," he muttered as he put his hand in his pocket and pulled out a key to the Victorian. He went to Olive's door but knocked instead of letting himself in with the key.

She opened the door, looking confused when she saw it was him. "I thought you had a poker game tonight and weren't— Wait, why are you knocking? Did you lose your key?"

The small piece of metal felt heavy in his hand. "Yeah, about that..."

"Aren't you coming in?" she asked and turned back toward the door.

"Um... I...think we should talk out here."

"Why? So the kitties won't overhear us?" She smiled but it flickered and died when he didn't return it. "Okay, but let me shut the door so they don't come running out."

He rubbed a hand across the back of his neck, trying to decide how to begin. Best to just plunge in.

"I realized today when I called you about my plans that you might be getting the wrong idea about this."

"This?" She drew her brows together in a puzzled frown.

"Us," he clarified. "About us."

"What about us?"

"I think we might each have a different explanation of what's been going on here." He stalked toward the far end of the porch.

"Oh?"

He swung back. "We're just having a bit of fun, right?"

"A bit of fun?" She sagged against the door she'd shut and shook her head.

Damn, but she surely had that look on her face and he felt like the worst person in the world. But he hadn't led her on, he argued with himself. He'd been up front about not wanting anything permanent. Hadn't he? He must have because that was always rule number one before he let anything get to the physical level.

She straightened away from the door and crossed her arms over her chest. "Then please tell me what we were doing."

"Having some fun?" Oh, God, he sounded like such an ass.

"Are you asking me or telling?"

"Sarcasm isn't a good look for you, Olive." Why was he baiting her? Did he want her to lash out and make this easier for him? "You knew before we… Before we became physically…in-involved that I don't do relationships."

"Physically involved? Oh, you mean before we made lo— No, wait! That wasn't what we did, was it? We had sex. Plain and simple. We made the beast with two backs. Did the dirty. Bumped uglies."

"Olive, stop." He gritted his teeth against the urge to take her in his arms, tell her it was all a misunderstanding. But if he let this go on, she'd expect more from him. More than he could give. He had his no relationships rule for a reason. Just because he was having trouble remembering those reasons every time he looked at her didn't mean they weren't valid.

"Don't turn what we shared into something ugly or clichéd," he blurted out when the silence between them stretched.

"But clichéd is exactly what it was."

"Look, I…" He searched his fevered brain for the right words.

"You know what? You're right. I don't know what it was, but I do know what it wasn't. Love. Except for me. I was the fool falling in love."

"Please don't."

"Don't what? Don't *fall*, fall in love? Don't plan on a future? Don't count on you to feel the same? Too late, Cal. I made the mistake of doing all those things."

"I'm sorry. I truly am," he said miserably.

"You know something, Cal Pope, I don't need you and I don't need your pity."

"Pity? Is that what you think this was about?"

Yes, that's exactly what this was about. What else was she supposed to think?

"What else was it about? You have this inflated hero complex and seem to think I need saving. But guess what? I don't. I can save myself."

"Good luck with that next time you have a mouse running around your house."

"Did I ask you to come bursting in? I would have handled it. I've survived thirty-three years without you. I can survive the rest of my life. I may not ever attend an international film festival or own art by Banksy—"

"Wait a minute. Why would you want to own a piece of street art?"

She waved a hand in the air. *Oh, God, Olive, what are you babbling about?* "It's nothing… It's just… just a movie I saw. Forget I said that."

"That's a pretty hard thing to forget."

"I'm sure you'll succeed if you give yourself up to it." She hated that she'd used something he'd said against him. She was no better than Kurt's sister and her snotty friends, who'd embarrassed her because she was ignorant when it came to the world of street artists. After that incident she'd done some research and watched *Exit Through the Gift Shop*. She never felt out of place or like she didn't belong with Cal and her friends, though. *Until now.* "But I'm going to be okay. I'm good enough the way I am." She had aimed her words like aiming an arrow and hitting a bull's-eye.

"I didn't mean to hurt you, Olive."

"And yet you did. But guess what? I'll get over it. I'll get over you because I'm a survivor. And what I'm feeling isn't your fault so don't give it another thought. I'm responsible for my own feelings."

"Olive, I did warn you before we even got involved that I wasn't a relationship guy."

"You're right and I accepted that." He was speaking the truth, but it didn't make this any easier. She still had whiplash from the about-face he'd done. What had she done?

She recalled their earlier conversation when she reminded him of their Friday night plans. They'd drifted into acting like a couple. Had he just noticed that and gotten spooked?

Well, she hadn't done anything wrong.

"A clean break might be best if that's how you feel," she told him.

The look on his face was almost comical. She might have laughed if her heart wasn't shattering into a million pieces. Was he going to miss her? Or the sex?

Maybe she should ask him. But, no, that was going to take more guts than she had at the moment.

It was going to be awkward enough seeing him across the street coming and going, knowing she had no right to ask what he was doing.

"I guess we'll just wave to one another from across the street."

He opened his mouth as if to speak, but shut it again. Turning on his heel, he headed toward his house.

She watched him until he'd walked into his house. Turning around she hugged herself and went back inside.

Both kittens crawled onto her lap and purred as if sensing she needed that.

She recalled that day he'd appeared at her door with a kitten in each hand.

How had she gotten this so wrong? Once again, she hadn't heeded warnings about getting involved with the wrong man.

Sighing, she buried her face in Mayhem's fur when the cat put her front paws on Olive's shoulder

Chapter Fifteen

Cal drove up and down the rows in the parking lot at the library, looking for a spot. He finally nabbed one, grateful he wouldn't have to park on the street and walk a block or two. They were drawing the raffle winners today, so the place was crowded. This was a culmination of all of Olive's hard work.

Sure, he'd been cochair and had done what was asked of him, but Olive's belief in Camp Life Launch had caused her to put her heart into the project.

Bracing himself mentally for being with Olive again, he walked into the community room at the library. He glanced around the crowded room but couldn't spot that unmistakable cascade of curls anywhere. He spotted Ellie and immediately went over to her.

"Where's Olive?" Cal demanded.

"She's not coming." The look Ellie gave him was a mixture of annoyance and pity.

"What do you mean 'not coming'?" He shook his head. She wouldn't miss this. She'd been anticipating it since the beginning.

"She didn't want to make things awkward for you," Ellie said.

She wouldn't forfeit being here tonight for him, would she? "Are you sure you didn't misunderstand?"

"All I know is she texted me, saying she wouldn't be attending tonight's ceremony." Ellie gave him a pointed look. "You really messed up. I have to check on something, but we'll talk later."

He sighed. "Is that a promise or a threat?"

She patted his arm. "A little of both."

This reminded him of the night Olive had bailed on the meeting. That night she'd been hurting and chose to suffer alone.

He hated the thought of her all alone in that big house. Was she—

"Got any ice cream, Mr. Cal?"

Cal turned to see David, the camper from Life Launch, coming to stand next to him.

"Hey, buddy, I didn't expect to see you here. I

thought you went home already." Cal did a fist bump with the boy.

"I did but Miss Olive arranged for me to come for another week after I messed up."

"How did you mess up?"

David shuffled his feet. "There was a family, the Burtons, who wanted to spend some time with me, to get to know me better, but I got scared and said some stupid stuff about not wanting to get adopted."

"Why would you sabotage your chances of getting a permanent placement?" Cal tried to keep the censure out of his voice, but him questioning David was probably censure enough in the boy's mind.

The boy hunched his shoulders forward. "Who's going to want to adopt someone my age? Everybody knows they all want cute little babies."

"Not everyone. If you don't put yourself out there to connect with people, it's a self-fulfilling prophecy."

David scrunched up his face. "What's that?"

It's like what he'd done with Olive. He'd been afraid of having an adult relationship with her, committing himself and putting his trust in her. So even when they'd drifted into one, anyway, he'd done all he could to sabotage it. As if to say, "See, I knew this wouldn't work." Maybe if he'd given it an honest chance, he'd still be with her. Then he could ask her to help with David.

You could ask her, anyway, a voice in his head

told him. Olive wasn't vindictive but generous to a fault. He thought of the ugly, half-dead flowers she'd dragged home from the nursery and—

"Mr. Pope? Are you okay?"

David's voice broke into his thoughts, and he shook his head. Deal with one thing at a time, he told himself. "Yeah, I'm fine. A self-fulfilling prophecy is when you think you don't have a chance at a permanent placement so you sabotage yourself and then say 'See, I knew it wouldn't happen.' You can't let what's happened in your past rule your life."

"But…"

"Not letting yourself trust anyone isn't any way to live." *Talk about pot, kettle.*

"Is that why you and Miss Olive aren't together anymore?"

Before Cal could question him, David shrugged. "I overheard the Wilsons talking about it."

Cal managed not to ask David what he'd overheard…barely.

"But if you trusted Miss Olive, why aren't you still together?"

"That's where you're wrong." And so was he. "I didn't trust Olive and that's why we're not together."

"So, you, ah, like did that self-prophecy thing to yourself?"

Cal chuckled, even though it hurt his chest. Hell, everything hurt these days. "Yeah, I guess I did."

David lifted his chin. "And what are you gonna

do about it? That's what Miss Olive asked me when I told her I deliberately misbehaved when I went to visit that family who wanted to get to know me better."

Cal's chuckle turned into a full-blown laugh. He reached out and gave the boy a playful shoulder shove. "If I promise to talk to Olive and apologize for my behavior, will you promise to give the Burtons another chance?"

David's Adam's apple bobbed as he swallowed. "That's partly why I came back. The Wilsons said meeting on neutral territory like the camp might help me feel more relaxed."

"And the Burtons are coming?" David nodded and Cal put his hand on the boy's shoulder. "Good, but you have to promise to at least give it a chance."

"And you'll promise to talk to Miss Olive and beg forgiveness?"

"Beg?" Cal lifted an eyebrow at the boy.

"I hear that's the key to a happy marriage."

"Who have you been talking to?"

The kid shrugged but color ran high in his cheeks. "I hear stuff."

Cal reached out and pulled David in for a neck hug. "Who have you been hearing this wisdom from?"

"I heard Mr. Brody telling someone to do that. He said big transgressions call for big apologies."

"I hope the Burtons realize what a great kid you are, David."

Cal shook hands with David and wished him luck. But before he could escape the celebration, Liam strolled over and clapped him on the shoulder.

"Just the man I wanted to see. I'll have you know, Ellie's been bending my ear the past few days, so I need to repay the favor," Liam said and grinned at Cal's grimace.

"If this is about—"

"Hell, you know it is. So, I'm going to impart some wisdom and you can learn from my mistakes." Liam sighed. "You can learn from me or spend the rest of your life in blissful ignorance."

"And if I choose blissful ignorance?" Cal asked.

"Then that's your choice, but I wanted you to know that I understand your fear because I, too, as hard as you may find this to believe, was afraid of a serious relationship with Ellie."

"What did you have to be afraid of?" Cal couldn't imagine his friend being afraid of his relationship with Ellie. They were so good together.

"A lot of things. I was afraid the cancer from her childhood would return. After cancer took my mom and a friend of mine, I saw it almost as this giant entity that could take away those I loved on a whim. I thought it was better to live without Ellie than to take a chance at losing her."

"You obviously changed your mind. So how did you get past that?"

"My dad helped me see reason."

"Yeah, I don't have one of those handy," he said drily.

"Quit being a jerk, Pope. And don't give me that look. I recognize jerk behavior because I was like that with Ellie."

Yeah, Cal had to agree he was being a jerk, but he couldn't help it. He hadn't been in charge of his emotions or actions since Olive had turned that smile on him. She had him tied in knots. "So how did your dad help? What great pearls of wisdom did he impart?"

"He told me to quit being a jerk," Liam said and laughed.

Despite the fraught situation and the knot in his gut, he chuckled. "Yeah, that sounds like Mac."

"I asked him how he was able to put himself out there again after Ma died and he basically said that he found something more important than the fear." Liam's gaze bounced around the room until he spotted his wife. "And Mac asked me if Ellie was that important thing. And now I'm asking you if Olive is that important thing for you."

Cal's chest contracted until he had difficulty breathing. Olive was the most important thing in his life. What had possessed him to think he could even contemplate living without her? She brought sunshine into his life. Without her, he was only existing, letting what his dad did rule his life. He might not ever forget what his father had done, but it was time to forgive and move on. He couldn't let the past ruin his future. Not if that future could involve Olive. He could even picture a few rug rats—the two-legged kind, this time—running around that rambling Victorian. He smiled at the thought. He might not have had a terrific example to model in his own dad, but he'd watched his friends enough to know how to do it right.

Liam patted him on the shoulder, much as he had done to David. "Only you can decide if she's worth it, but I can safely recommend taking that leap of faith. Ellie and the kids are worth it…all of it."

Cal nodded, and he'd bet his Adam's apple was bobbing as much as David's had. "McBride? Tell Mac thanks for me."

Liam nodded. "And, Cal? If you tell anyone we had a conversation about *feelings*, you're toast."

Cal laughed. "Gotcha."

Olive's declaration of love played on a continuous loop in his head as he drove off. Had she meant it? He suspected she did, or she wouldn't have admitted it. She wasn't the type to say something just to make him feel bad. But even if it was true then, was it true now?

He could only pray that it was because Olive was definitely the most important person in his life. And he'd do anything—even move past the pain of his childhood—to make her smile. And if she forgave him, he knew he'd spend the rest of his life trying to create a safe, happy environment for themselves, the cats and any other creatures they might welcome into their home. Human or not.

Chapter Sixteen

Olive checked her watch and sighed. Missing tonight's ceremony was probably immature, an overreaction to breaking things off with Cal. But the wound was still fresh. She would never stop wanting a family of her own, but she needed to live her life. Appreciate what she did have in that life. "I'm enough," she whispered.

She'd be that old cat lady. Weird and fun-loving Aunt Olive to her friends' children. She'd look into volunteering at Mary and Brody's camp. She'd be a model for those kids. Show them that you could come through the system and still succeed. If she wasn't enough for herself, what would she be teaching those young people? Those little ones who looked up to her. She wanted to set a good example for them. Help them make good decisions. She told them they were worthy whether or not someone adopted them.

Now it was time to take her own advice.

The door chime startled her out of her morose thoughts. As much as she loved the restored Victorian doorbell, a wave of sadness washed over her as it brought back memories of the night Cal had worked to restore it. The kittens had freaked out at the noise each time he tested it and had scrambled over one another to find a hiding place. She and Cal had laughed at their feline antics and that laughter had led to— *Don't go there. And no scrambling to hide, either.* Instead she went and opened the door.

As if anticipating her reaction, Cal stuck his foot in the door.

"What did you want?" she asked.

"To grovel."

Her heart began to beat faster at his words. She hated that she was still vulnerable to her feelings for him.

"I'd rather do it inside, especially if it involves me dropping to my knees to beg, but I'll do it out here for all to see if that's what you want," he told her.

She swung the door open and walked into the front parlor. She crossed her arms over her chest. She didn't need to make this easy for him. "What did you want?"

"In a perfect world, I'd be able to tell you exactly when it happened."

Had he been drinking? She scrunched up her face. "When exactly what happened?"

"When I fell in love with you. I'm not sure I can pinpoint *exactly*, but I know it must have started when you stood in front of me and—"

"Wait! You love me?" Her heart threatened to pound out of her chest.

"That's what I'm saying."

"Could—could you say it again? Use the words again. Please." Afraid she might be hallucinating, she needed to hear them again.

He pressed a hand to his chest as if taking a pledge. "I love you, Olive Downing. With all my heart and soul. I was a goner when you defended weeds."

"I wasn't defending them. Just pointing out that they sometimes get a bad rap."

"Whatever you did, it made me want to kiss you."

"But that was barely a peck."

"I was afraid if I started, I might not have wanted to stop. And that proved to be true."

She was starting to feel giddy. Was this what pure happiness felt like?

"We're going to have lots of time to debate that first kiss," he said.

"What's that supposed to mean." Had she even

heard that right? Her thoughts, her feelings, everything felt chaotic.

"It means I'm going to be kissing you for the rest of my life."

"Even when we're old and gray." She smiled as it started to sink in that this was real. Cal loved her.

"Especially then. We'll embarrass the great-grandkids with overt displays of affection."

He reached for her and took her into his arms, slowly, gently, as if afraid she'd bolt, but she had no plans for going anywhere except into those loving arms.

"Wow. You really are planning ahead." She edged closer.

He eased her against him. "You bet. I know the key to a happy marriage."

"Overt displays of affection?" She met his gaze.

He grinned. "And knowing when to beg for forgiveness."

A thought occurred to her, and she frowned. "Are you sure about this? You were afraid to trust me. How do I know that you won't do that again?"

He rested his forehead against hers. "Because I may not be the smartest guy in the room, but I am a fast learner."

"And what did you learn?"

He sighed, his breath warm on her face. "I learned that I really, really, really hate my life without you in it. If having you in my life means I need to step off the cliff without a net, then I'll do it."

"That's pretty much what it feels like, doesn't it?" She wanted him to know she understood.

"Pretty much, but you'll get used to it."

"So now you're giving me advice about trust?"

He shook his head. "I never had any problems trusting you."

"Didn't appear that way to me." Why was she arguing? *Because I need to be sure*, her inner voice answered.

"I have always trusted you, Olive. It was myself I didn't trust. I let what my father did undermine my trust in myself. It's taken me twenty years to figure that out, but I did, thanks to you. I shudder to think what my life would have been like without you in it."

"Pretty boring, I would say," she teased.

He grew still, serious. "Thank you for rescuing me."

"Me?" She shook her head. "You were the one always riding to my rescue."

"Those were nothing compared to how you've rescued me, Olive."

"I don't understand."

He brushed a lock of curly hair behind her ear. "You rescued me, not from spiderwebs or field mice, but from a solitary existence. You've given me more than I could ever imagine for myself.

"I want to walk through this life with you, Olive. You and me, side by side. What do you say?"

She hugged him. "Yes! I say yes."

He picked her up and twirled her in a circle.

Their friends all congratulated themselves on bringing the newly engaged couple together. They all wanted to take credit for knowing they belonged together.

Two weeks after their reconciliation, Cal handed her a package wrapped in brown kraft paper. Now that he was faced with her unwrapping it, he wondered if she'd understand the gesture. Would she laugh, think his gesture was silly?

He shuffled his feet. "It's really—"

"Absolutely wonderful," she exclaimed as she held the framed litho print out in front of her. "It's a Banksy, right?"

Warmth rose in his face. "Yeah. Not an original but I hope you like it."

"I love it."

She set it aside and threw her arms around him. "It's perfect."

And so worth the effort if this was the result. Her in his arms. "I can't give you the world, Olive, but I'd like to try."

"You've given me something better. You've demonstrated how much you love me."

"By giving you a Banksy print?"

"By giving me kittens and driving me to the ER

and all the other hundreds of things you've done to demonstrate how much you care."

He leaned over and gave her a kiss. "I guess I'm a pretty nice guy."

"You're the best," she said and looped her arm around his neck to continue what he'd started.

His phone dinged to indicate a text before the kiss could turn into the kind that promised more.

"I'm on call," he said, and she took a step back.

"Work?" she asked as she bent down to take a piece of the paper wrapping out of Mayhem's mouth.

He shook his head, glancing up grinning. "David."

She dropped the paper, and the kitten ran off with it. "David from the camp?"

"That's the one."

"What did he want?"

He held up his phone and turned the display toward her. "To let me know the Burtons have started the paperwork to adopt him."

"Oh, that's wonderful. But why did he text you?"

He shrugged but couldn't stop the warmth rising in him. "Well, I may have encouraged him to take a chance at happiness."

She took the phone from his hand and set it on an end table. "Have I told you lately how much I love you?"

"Not in the past hour."

She hugged him. "So, I'm due."

"I'd say past due." He lowered his head to capture those enticing lips again.

She pulled away before he could make contact. "And what about you? Don't you have something to say?"

"I love you, Olive. More than I could ever imagine."

And he sealed the declaration with a kiss.

Epilogue

Three years later

Cal was sweeping the floor in front of the litter box. Mischief and Mayhem were no longer kittens and spent their days sleeping more than they played, but the pair was still bringing joy to their lives.

When Olive first suspected she could be pregnant, he'd insisted on litter-box duty. He'd read about some disease that could affect pregnant women who cleaned up after cats.

They'd been married for two years, and Cal had to admit those were the happiest of his life. After much debate, they'd postponed reopening the B and B. He'd sold his place for a tidy profit, and they'd plowed the money into renovating the Victorian. They'd brought it back to its former glory and Cal reveled in the joy on his wife's face when she admired all their hard work.

Little things, such as an in-drawer bread box, still brought her joy. As did dragging home half-dead plants and nurturing them until they blossomed.

He chuckled. That's basically what she'd done to him.

"Cal?"

"Coming." He threw the bag into the trash and quickly washed his hands before going in search of his wife.

He found her standing in a puddle in the hallway. It was time. His heart pounded, not with dread but excitement. He was looking forward to raising children with Olive. He only hoped they inherited her sunny disposition. And maybe her hair.

He picked up the small suitcase he'd insisted be left by the door and took her arm in his.

He tried to urge her toward the door but Olive planted her feet on the hardwood floor in the Victorian's entryway and refused to budge.

"Are you sure about this?" she asked.

Cal hooted a laugh. One thing he'd learned about his wife in the past three years was that for all of her bravado, she was a bundle of nerves about certain things. Dark basements, spiders, mice, childbirth. "Absolutely positive. Just like that pregnancy test."

"But…" She shook her head, gnawing on her lower lip.

He swallowed his frustration. If she had fears, it was up to him to reassure her. "Talk to me, Olive."

"It's just—you never wanted kids. Or a wife."

"Olive, sweetheart, I love you…hopelessly, helplessly, endlessly. I married you because I wanted to spend my life with you. And now we're going to be starting our family. And I want that, too.

"Besides, that positive test was nine months ago." He put his arms around her and tried shooing her toward the door. "And didn't your water just break?"

"Yes, but—"

"No *buts*. Let's go. And you put a spell on me."

"What kind of spell?"

"The best kind. The kind that guarantees a lifetime of happiness."

"You mean that?" She lifted her gaze to his.

"More than I have ever meant anything in my life."

"But—"

"Olive, sweetheart, can we continue this discussion in the car? On the way to the hospital. I'd really like for our baby to be born in a hospital."

"But your training—"

"Did not include childbirth. If you've stepped on an IED or been shot or had shrapnel wounds, I'm your guy, but babies? Uh-uh. Let's get this show on the road. I can't wait to meet our son."

And he meant every word. Another thing he'd learned in the past three years was that it was better to look forward than backward. The past could inform them, but it should never prevent them from embracing the present.

And that's what he'd been doing. Embracing every day with Olive and looking ahead to their future, letting go of all the bitterness and disappointments from the past.

Some twenty hours later, Cal sat in the chair next to Olive's hospital bed, holding his newborn son and looking at him, his eyes full of wonder and shiny with tears. "He's beautiful."

"I think you mean handsome." She smiled and settled back against the pillows. She was physically drained and was doing her best to keep her eyes open. She didn't want to miss a moment of watching Cal bond with their baby boy.

"Hey, there, young man. I'm your dad and you're going to have to be very patient with me because I'm probably going to make plenty of mistakes."

"Cal!" Her eyes flew open. "You're going to be a wonderful dad."

He smiled, then turned back to their son. "But I can promise you this," he continued as if she hadn't spoken. "I picked the best woman in the whole wide world to be your mommy, so things are going to be fine. For all of us."

* * * * *

WE HOPE YOU ENJOYED
THIS BOOK FROM

◆ HARLEQUIN

SPECIAL
EDITION

Believe in love. Overcome obstacles. Find happiness.

Relate to finding comfort and strength in the
support of loved ones and enjoy the journey
no matter what life throws your way.

6 NEW BOOKS AVAILABLE EVERY MONTH!

#2899 CINDERELLA NEXT DOOR

The Fortunes of Texas: The Wedding Gift
by Nancy Robards Thompson

High school teacher and aspiring artist Ginny Sanders knows she is not Draper Fortune's type. Content to admire her fabulous and flirty new neighbor from a distance, she is stunned when he asks her out. Draper is charmed by the sensitive teacher, but when he learns why she doesn't date, he must decide if he can be the man she needs...

#2900 HEIR TO THE RANCH

Dawson Family Ranch • by Melissa Senate

The more Gavin Dawson shirks his new role, the more irate Lily Gold gets. The very pregnant single mom-to-be is determined to make her new boss see the value in his late father's legacy—her livelihood and her home depend on it! But Gavin's plan to ignore his inheritance and Lily—*and* his growing attraction to her—is proving to be impossible...

#2901 CAPTIVATED BY THE COWGIRL

Match Made in Haven • by Brenda Harlen

Devin Blake is a natural loner, but when rancher Claire Lamontagne makes the first move, he finds himself wondering if he's as content as he thought he was. Is Devin ready to trade his solitary life for a future with the cowgirl tempting him to take a chance on love?

#2902 MORE THAN A TEMPORARY FAMILY

Furever Yours • by Marie Ferrarella

A visit with family was just what Josie Whitaker needed to put her marriage behind her. Horseback-riding lessons were an added bonus. But her instructor, Declan Hoyt, is dealing with his moody teenage niece. The divorced single mom knows just how to help and offers to teach Declan a thing or two about parenting—never expecting a romance to spark with the younger rancher!

#2903 LAST CHANCE ON MOONLIGHT RIDGE

Top Dog Dude Ranch • by Catherine Mann

Their love wasn't in doubt, but fertility issues and money problems have left Hollie and Jacob O'Brien's marriage in shambles. So once the spring wedding season at their Tennessee mountain ranch is over, they'll part ways. Until Jacob is inspired to romance Hollie and her long-buried maternal instincts are revived by four orphaned children visiting the ranch. Will their future together be resurrected, too?

#2904 AN UNEXPECTED COWBOY

Sutton's Place • by Shannon Stacey

Lone-wolf cowboy Irish is no stranger to long, lonely nights. But somehow Mallory Sutton tugs on his heartstrings. The feisty single mom is struggling to balance it all—and challenging Irish's perception of what he has to offer. But will their unexpected connection keep Irish in town...or end in heartbreak for Mallory and her kids?

SPECIAL EXCERPT FROM

HQN

Mariella Jacob was one of the world's premier bridal designers. One viral PR disaster later, she's trying to get her torpedoed career back on track in small-town Magnolia, North Carolina. With a second-hand store and a new business venture helping her friends turn the Wildflower Inn into a wedding venue, Mariella is finally putting at least one mistake behind her. Until that mistake—in the glowering, handsome form of Alex Ralsten—moves to Magnolia too...

Read on for a sneak preview of
Wedding Season,
the next book in USA TODAY bestselling author Michelle Major's Carolina Girls series!

"You still don't belong here." Mariella crossed her arms over her chest, and Alex commanded himself not to notice her body, perfect as it was.

"That makes two of us, and yet here we are."

"I was here first," she muttered. He'd heard the argument before, but it didn't sway him.

"You're not running me off, Mariella. I needed a fresh start, and this is the place I've picked for my home."

"My plan was to leave the past behind me. You are a physical reminder of so many mistakes I've made."

"I can't say that upsets me too much," he lied. It didn't make sense, but he hated that he made her so uncomfortable. Hated even more that sometimes he'd purposely drive by her shop to get a glimpse of her through the picture window. Talk about a glutton for punishment.

She let out a low growl. "You are an infuriating man. Stubborn and callous. I don't even know if you have a heart."

"Funny." He kept his voice steady even as memories flooded him, making his head pound. "That's the rationale Amber gave me for why she cheated with your fiancé. My lack of emotions pushed her into his arms. What was his excuse?"

She looked out at the street for nearly a minute, and Alex wondered if she was even going to answer. He followed her gaze to the park across the street, situated in the center of the town. There were kids at the playground and several families walking dogs on the path that circled the perimeter. Magnolia was the perfect place to raise a family.

If a person had the heart to be that kind of a man—the type who married the woman he loved and set out to be a good husband and father. Alex wasn't cut out for a family, but he liked it in the small coastal town just the same.

"I was too committed to my job," she said suddenly and so quietly he almost missed it.

"Ironic since it was your job that introduced him to Amber."

"Yeah." She made a face. "This is what I'm talking about, Alex. A past I don't want to revisit."

"Then stay away from me, Mariella," he advised. "Because I'm not going anywhere."

"Then maybe I will," she said and walked away.

Don't miss
Wedding Season *by Michelle Major,*
available May 2022 wherever
HQN books and ebooks are sold.

HQNBooks.com